KINKY GIRLS

KINKY GIRLS

A COLLECTION OF TWENTY EROTIC STORIES

EDITED BY

MIRANDA FORBES

Published by Accent Press Ltd – 2011
ISBN 9781907016561

Printed and bound in the UK

Cover design by
Zipline Creative

Contents

A Member of the Profession
by Angel Propps

'You don't understand,' I said to the blank-faced man behind the counter at the jewellery store. 'I need to return this ring. I am no longer engaged and … And what could I say? My bastard ex-fiancé had decided to dump me three weeks before our wedding and head off to Europe for a few months with every dollar in our joint bank account. The bills from the wedding had all come due and even after my parents had given what they could I had been stuck with cancellation fees and costs that were eating away every dollar I could lay my fingers on. I was broke and desperate and I wanted the man behind the counter to allow me to return the ring so I could at least have a little money in my pocket.

'No,' the thin and prissy-faced man said stuffily, 'You don't understand. You cannot return that ring for a refund because it did not come from this store.' He said that last with a look of utter distaste that would have been funny on any other day.

'I don't understand,' I said angrily. 'What do you mean it did not come from here? Here is the box and it says …'

'No matter what the box says, the ring did not come from here. That is not even a diamond, it is a cubic zirconia.'

I stared at him and then down at the ring he had lain on the counter like it would dirty his hand if he touched it too long. A stunning blonde stood at the long counter pretending not to hear us and I had enough time to wonder if she was there to pick out her own ring before I burst into tears. I could not help it, I was just a wreck. I grabbed the box that held the ring the bastard had given me and went out their door reflecting bitterly that he had certainly pulled a fast one on me. I had a bum ring and he had all the checking account money. I was trying to find ways to pay for everything and he was walking across good old Paris.

'Wait,' a husky voice said from behind me. I spun around and there she was; a tall, thin beauty in full make-up and dangerous red stilettos and a red and white designer sundress that cost more than my entire wardrobe. It was barely noon. I stood there and she came closer, I could smell the musky bitterness of her perfume, see the perfectly glossed streaks in her honey and platinum hair.

'What do you want?' I could hear the tiredness in my voice.

'I couldn't help but overhear. I was wondering … I could … if you would like to make some money I could help you with that.'

I stared at her. She looked like a model or a life sized doll. I couldn't figure out what she wanted with me so I just asked, 'What do you mean?'

We were standing outside the glass windows of the jewellery store and she took my arm and guided me out of the jeweller's vision before she spoke. 'I like sex,' she said bluntly, 'I like to fuck. I don't want a relationship or to be bothered with dinner and dancing or sweet words. I don't like games; I just want to get laid. If you want to let me fuck you I will pay you $1,000.'

I burst into laughter. I mean it had to be a joke. For one second I actually looked around to see if I could spot the camera crew. There I stood, all five foot five and one hundred and fifty four pounds of me. Dark brown hair that hung to my shoulders, a face that was pretty when it wasn't so worried-looking. Stubborn curves of both hip and tits and thick thighs that always seemed to draw attention. Nothing

2

special. I mean Demi Moore might get hit on like that but me?

'OK, $2,000.'

She wasn't joking. I stood there looking at her face and the thing that kept me rooted to the spot was that simple truth. She meant it. She wanted to pay me two grand to fuck me.

'I'm not gay.'

'Neither am I. I am married, though, to a 74-year-old bastard who has a private eye who follows me as a career so there's no way I can talk to men. If I could I would, believe it.'

I knew it was insane. I mean who does that kind of thing? But I kept thinking of the way the jerk behind the jewellery store counter had been fawning over her when I walked in. I kept looking at the beauty shopped hair and the perfect toenails peeking from the open toes of her stilettos. I kept thinking how much I could get done with two grand.

'Fuck it,' I said, 'I'm in.'

Half an hour later I was wondering if I was crazy all over again. She had put me in her limo's plushy interior and we had chatted casually. She had whispered that there was a camera and the driver was nosy and a spy to boot so we pretended to be old college friends who had run into each other again.

We had not been inside her luxurious condominium for ten minutes before I was tied to her bed. Literally. She had me stripped bare, shoved down onto the mattress and restrained so fast I did not know what hit me. I was flat on my back with my legs hoisted high and tied to the bed posts so that they were wide open and my ass cheeks were exposed. My arms were outstretched and also tied while a hard red ball gag was shoved in between my lips before I could even think.

'Now we are ready to fuck,' she purred and I stared as she took the dress off. Under it she was both unbelievably

3

beautiful and naked. Her tits were small but firm, her ass curved upwards and her belly in. Her ribs stuck out and her pussy was clean shaven. I had to fight to breathe I was so scared but turned on all at the same time. 'You better be worth my money, bitch,' she added and I screamed behind the gag as she slapped my ass cheeks with one dainty hand.

The spanking went on for a long time. At first I quivered and shrieked, tried to get away but then the pain faded and a boiling lust ignited in my belly. I could feel come dripping down the crack of my ass and dropping onto the bed. My eyes rolled back in my head and I whimpered with pleasure when she pushed a finger deep inside me.

'You like that?' She asked and then there were more fingers and her thumb was rubbing my clit fiercely, making me beg helplessly. I could feel how swollen and hard my clit was and she laughed as she took her hand away from me and left me straining upwards in need.

She laughed again, a musical tinkle of sound and walked away from the bed. I could hear the faint click of her stilettos as she moved. Fear caused me to look over but I almost instantly wished I hadn't. She had a harness, something I had only ever seen on the pornos the bastard had liked so much and she was placing this gigantic cock in it, wriggling to get it just right and when she gave a happy sigh and clicked her way back to the bed I started to beg.

'I can't understand you,' she said coolly, 'I don't speak poverty. Now if you want this to stop it will, but you won't get a dime from me, do you understand?'

Rage and shame flooded my chest but my pussy was still dripping. I could not believe it. I could not possibly want that humiliation. I tried to form the words fuck you but the gag would not allow me to speak. She placed a tiny silver bell in my right hand and said, 'You ring that bell, bitch, if you want to quit. Do you get it?'

'Mhmmm uhhh,' I got out and she climbed up into the bed, deliberately letting that cock slide across my belly, my

4

chest and then she slapped me across the face with her tiny hand and rubbed that cock against the gag and my lips.

'Bet you want me, you slummy little whore,' she said and I groaned. 'I bet you wish you could afford something as nice as this.' I watched as her hands rubbed her tits, pinched at her nipples and raised them into hard pink peaks, 'You are not good enough to taste my pussy. You will never be good enough for me. '

I burst into tears and she backed away from my face so she could bite and suck at my large and dark nipples. They rose up, begging for her rough attention and she slapped them, twisted and bit them again and again until I screamed in misery.

I came screaming and with her mouth on my aching nipples. I came wondering if this crazy doll baby woman was going to kill me. I came wondering if I even gave a shit if I did get killed. The way I was coming might have been worth it.

'I am going to fuck you until you beg me to stop,' she said and I had time to take one breath before she was inside me. That cock was enormous and I could feel it stretching me open wider and wider. She shoved it in as hard as she could while I lay there helpless under her. I could feel tears running down my cheeks and she laughed again as those tears streaked my face and ran down my chin. 'Feels good doesn't it, you cheap bitch? You like that?'

I nodded. Well, I did like it. I had never done anything like it, felt anything like it and I didn't want it to end. Her perfect body slapped against mine as she fucked me. Her tiny tits bounced and her razor sharp hip bones slammed cruelly against the inside of my thighs. Her hands twisted into my hair and she yanked my head up, forcing me to look into her eyes as she brutally used my cunt.

'You better not come again. If you do, I am gonna pull this cock out of your cunt and stuff it in your asshole. Do you hear me?'

'Yes!' I screamed and she laughed at my muffled agreement.

I had to look at her and she knew it. She locked her eyes on to mine and shoved herself into me harder and faster, grinding and thrusting until my pussy was soaked and sore. She reached over to the pillow and picked up the odd shaped object that she had laid there and with a flick of her wrist it began to purr. I screamed and tried to get away but she had tied me well. I could not escape from the cock, from the powerful pulsing hum of the vibrator as she worked it against my clit.

'Don't come, you slut,' she yelled at me. She had let go of my hair and she used her free hand to slap me lightly across the face again even as she fucked me even deeper than ever before.

'I won't,' I sobbed behind my restraint but she ignored it and pushed the vibrator harder against the throbbing knot of my clit. It was too much to take. She kept yelling for me not to come and the cock was fucking me so good, it felt so fucking right inside me. The vibrator purred. She fucked my pussy. I wanted to stay right there for ever.

'If you come it's going in your ass,' she warned and I arched helplessly upwards, 'I mean it, you are gonna get fucked in the ass and it will hurt. Is that what you want?'

Please let me come, I thought as I tried to arch my ass higher. I wanted to feel every inch of that cock, wanted to take every bit of it and the vibrator was stimulating me to the point I was nearly crazy with lust. I wanted to come and I wanted her to fuck me in the ass. I loved anal, something she obviously didn't know and I was glad she didn't. I had the feeling if she knew she would not have wanted to do it so badly.

'Don't come,' she said again and I did. I whimpered and twisted, slobbering and drooling down my chin as she used me roughly. I knew she had turned me into a slave to her twisted game. I didn't give a shit, I wanted it.

'You bitch you knew better than that,' she said and then she withdrew from my cunt. I could feel come spooling and pooling down my thighs and I screamed once, then closed my eyes in complete ecstasy as she went inside my willing ass. I lifted myself, shoving myself up higher and resting on my shoulders so she could get in deeper. She laughed and slapped me again, a light little love tap that stung against my right cheek.

I have no idea how long she fucked me. I know I came over and over and I could tell when she did by the way she went faster and harder into me and then stopped, breathing deeply and whimpering. The sunlight drifted across the bed as she collapsed on top of me, groans coming from between her lips.

I would have held her but she did not untie me. That she did not want comfort was obvious anyway, she rested for a moment and then got off me. As soon as she had her breath she led me to a large, marble accented bathroom and we got into a standing shower together. She soaped me and I soaped her, the rich lather smelled of lilacs and the towels we dried with were thick and fluffy. I would have loved to simply bask in the decadence of it but she had grown tired and slightly irritated by that time.

At the front door, while I waited for her driver to bring her car around so I could go back to the jewellery store and retrieve mine, she handed me the two grand as well as an extra five crisp $100 bills.

'As a tip,' she said as I looked at her. 'Listen, if you want … well I have friends in the same position. Every once in a while they like … you know … to be serviced. None of us want women who look or live like us. We don't want anyone in our crowd, we need …'

She didn't finish. She didn't need to. It was easy to see that what she wanted was to be the one in charge sometimes. I wondered how often she felt as powerless and helpless as I had felt beneath her in that bed. How often she had lain beneath that old bastard of hers feeling trapped and used. We weren't that different really, she was doing what she had to do to make her lifestyle possible and I had just sold myself in the same way. The real differences were that I got to leave and go out and live my real life while she had to stay there. And I had fucking loved everything she had done to me.

'I'm in,' I said again, and she grinned and gave me an almost tender kiss on the cheek.

That was six months ago. I have met a few of her friends and have had a lot of fun with them. They are all gorgeous, kinky fuck-crazy women who like to be visited by the old college friend. Their husbands think I am the nerdy poor girl who went to school on scholarships and they laugh when they see me coming. I laugh too because they do not know that when their backs are turned their wives are giving me the pussy they pay for.

Am I a whore? You would probably say so. I don't care. Everyone sells themselves in one way or another. Everyone is a whore. Some of us just like it more.

Arjun's Wedding
by Carmel Lockyer

My breasts had been wrapped around with shiny black
bondage tape – so bound and criss-crossed that they offered
themselves up in defiance of gravity. Both wrists too were
fastened, although a silky tether ran between them and the
bed-head, giving me a little scope to move around. That
tether had been a silk scarf around my shoulders an hour
ago, providing a rich purple contrast to my lavender dress.

My legs were free, able to kick out if I wanted to, or
spread wide if that was my preference, and everything else
that was happening was inclining me towards the spreading
option, although I was fighting it for as long as possible
because I wanted to prolong my current pleasure in the
situation.

"Everything else" was a dark head that was dipping over
my body, now nipping my belly with its teeth, then gently
nuzzling my neck, then allowing its long black hair to trail
across my breasts. It was strong hands, now pinching the
skin of my upper arms so I shivered in excitement, then
rubbing flat warm palms over my already aching nipples.
"Everything else" was just 20 years old, all male, all mine,
and … heading for the bedroom door.

'Wait!' My voice came out as a squeak.

He turned and grinned at me. 'Quiet, Meli. I'm needed at
the wedding. Don't worry, I'll be back soon. You won't
even miss me.'

I watched the door swing closed behind him and

wondered how the hell I was going to explain my situation if some wedding guest wandered into the room by mistake. My body began to cool and goose pimples rose on my breasts and thighs. Not miss him? I was aching for him already. I lay in the soft light from the bedside lamps and wondered quite how I'd got myself into this.

Arjun was my ex's best mate. When Hilad and I split, Arjun stayed in touch, just the occasional phone call, stuff like that, and then one day this red and gold card appeared in the post, all curly writing and bling, and the only thing I could pick out was his name. So I called him.

'Melinda.' He always made my name sound exotic, the way he said it. 'You got your invitation?'

'Invitation to what?'

'My wedding!'

Well that was a bit of a shock. 'Um … arranged wedding?' I asked, then I could have bitten my tongue off. Tactless or what?

'Um … yeah, hang on.' I heard him close a door, then his voice dropped. 'Sort of, anyway. Vidya's matchmaker contacted my family, but we've been spending time together, sort of informally, and we're, like, totally compatible.'

I giggled, Arjun was outrageous.

'What does she do for a living?'

'She's an Ayurvedic therapist, very hands-on.'

I giggled again, then asked the difficult question. 'Will he be there?'

'Look, Meli, you're my friend now. If Hilad and his new lady are there, so what? It's gonna be in a big hotel so there's plenty of chance to get away from him if you want.'

'Yeah …' I wasn't convinced though. I didn't think I wanted to see Hilad and the fiancé picked out by his mum to be a good Asian wife. But somehow, Arjun made me promise to attend and even said he'd send his Uncle Krishna to collect me on the day, so there was no getting out of it.

I looked in the mirror. White pasty skin looked back at me and there was nothing exotic about that. I wasn't a glacial Nordic beauty or Russian Ice Queen, I was just a boring brunette Brit. I pinched my upper arm hard, watching the pale flesh turn pink and fade again. 'Fake tan,' I said aloud, and rang the local tanning parlour.

Two days later, six tones darker, and one set of acrylic nails into the bargain, I tried to put together an outfit. A fusion wedding in Birmingham in April – even Trinny and Susannah would struggle to say what to wear. Add in the need for it to be 'ex-boyfriend impressing without being slutty' and 'acceptable to a bunch of elderly Asian women' as twin criteria for success and it began to look like mission impossible. I was almost resigned to wearing the burgundy salwar kameez I'd bought for last Diwali, when I'd expected Hilad to introduce me to his family. Instead, he'd rung me the night before and told me his father was very ill and the family thought it was time he settled down.

'So?' I said.

'So a matchmaker in India is finding me a wife. My father will see my bride before he dies.'

Just like that. End of relationship. End of the best sex I'd ever had. End of sharing my bed several nights a week with a man who seemed to have no fear of being emasculated, who loved sex toys as much as I did, who was prepared to dress up, drag up, role-play or act out any fantasy that either of us could come up with. Hilad had been the dream lover and like a dream he'd vanished into the cold light of reality. That was six months ago and I'd heard through Arjun that a young woman from Mumbai had been invited to come to England to meet Hilad's family – and she hadn't gone back, although no wedding had been arranged yet, or no wedding that Arjun had told me about. Instead he was the one getting married.

I rang him. 'Look, Arjun, it's really nice of you to invite

11

me but I have nothing to wear and anyway, I won't know anybody there or have a clue what to do – I really think …'

He cut me off by talking across me. 'Melinda, you're going to love Vidya and she's going to love you. A Hindu wedding takes all day, and is mainly standing around and gossiping and you're great at that. And if you're really worried about what to wear, I'll send Uncle Krishna to take you shopping. He knows Birmingham like the back of his hand – he's a taxi driver, you know.'

I sighed. There was a certain temptation to seeing Hilad again and getting a glance at his "new lady" as Arjun put it. 'Well OK, but if I can't find something good to wear I'm not coming, right?'

'Right. Can you take a morning off work? Taxi business is always quieter in the morning, you know.'

So I'd ended up being talked round by Arjun again, and now I was going shopping with his uncle – what fun that would be. Not. I'd met a couple of Hilad's uncles in the past; they were nice men, but barrel-bodied and hairy, fat wrists carrying flashy watches and shiny leather loafers on their small nimble feet. I'd joked to Hilad that he'd end up like them and he'd said, 'No way, Meli, I'll buy a corset to keep my waist and have my chest waxed.' And then he'd taken me to Pussy Galore and bought me the sexiest red patent leather corset I'd ever seen, saying that he'd want it back for himself one day, to make sure he didn't turn into his uncles.

I had to stop thinking about Hilad. The problem was that I'd had no meaningful relationship, except with a rabbit vibrator, since we'd split, and I was all too aware that love and marriage ended up in bed, which was a place I'd found to be cold and lonely since I'd lost Hilad.

OK, so substitute sex was all I was going to get. I pulled off the salwar and dragged the toy chest out from under my bed. It was packed with things I'd bought for Hilad or he'd bought for me, or we'd chosen together, giggling over the catalogues and online sex shops we'd browsed together. Top of the heap was a big deep blue dildo that he'd used on me hundreds of times, making me gasp as it entered me, filling me to a point that was almost unbearable, and then suddenly switching over into massive banging pleasure that made my fillings rattle as he pumped the big baby deeper until I plunged into orgasm.

Big Blue wasn't going to work for me as a solo job. I dug a bit deeper and found a set of bondage gear we'd used for weeks on end: soft leather cuffs for wrist and ankle that fastened to my bedposts. We'd taken it in turns to wear the restraints, one of us submitting to everything the other one could devise to cause pleasure. Hilad's greatest discovery had been that a gentle spanking on my buttocks made me so aroused I would beg and plead for him to fuck me.

Mine had been that unlike most people, Hilad loved to have his feet tickled and could be sent into quivering ecstasy if I drew a feather across his toes. He'd never actually come when I did it, but he'd got very close and then, when I mounted him he'd just explode into whatever kinky new condom we were trying on that occasion. Happy days.

And there, under some dressing-up clothes, was a lovely surprise. We'd bought the black glass dildo with a stopper back when we first got together but we were always too impatient to use it as it should be used, so it had slipped to the bottom of the box and I'd forgotten all about it. I lifted it, admiring its elegant shape and then carried it to the bathroom where I filled it with warm water and replaced the stopper.

Back on the bed, I lubed the glass well with my favourite "tingle" gel and lay back, eyes closed as I slipped the hot hardness inside me, imagining it was somebody else's hands doing the work of manipulating the slick surface in and out until I came.

It wasn't a pleasure, it was a necessity, like sneezing or coughing, so when the tremors of orgasm had passed I started again, working the dildo until my hand began to ache and my thigh muscles twitched with exhaustion. Then I relaxed, cradling the cooling glass vessel against my breasts, and wondered if I'd ever again have the kind of fun I'd had with Hilad.

Next morning, I was still sipping coffee when the doorbell rang. Uncle Krishna was early. I pulled open the door and stared. There was a boy on my doorstep. But what a boy! Not tall, but slim, with dark hair tied back in a ponytail, a pure white Armani shirt and tight black jeans, a smile like a slice of heaven … he could have made a fortune as a male stripper, or been a contender for Bollywood hero status. I think I probably sighed.

'Melinda Carson?'

I nodded. He held out his hand. 'I'm Krishna, Arjun's uncle.'

I spluttered into my coffee, felt it head up the back of my nose and panicked. Don't let me dribble coffee down my nose in front of this Indian god! So I ran back to the bathroom, leaving the flat door wide open, and stood there with a towel over my head and my face tipped back until I was sure all risk of a nose fountain had passed.

When I went back into the kitchen, Krishna was sitting at my breakfast bar.

'You're Arjun's uncle?' It was all I could think of to say.

'Yeah, I know. Mad innit? My dad is his eldest brother. I was one of those menopausal babies, so he was already in double figures when I was born.'

'And you're a taxi driver?'

Krishna grinned again. 'Manner of speaking. Actually I'm not – the insurance for me to drive a cab at my age would be mega-high. But at college I developed some new software to help dispatch cabs. Found a partner to invest in it and we set up a cab business – so although I don't generally drive, I do get out with the drivers to see how it's working.

14

We're hoping one of the big sat nav companies will buy the programme and make us rich, once we've ironed all the bugs out.'

My head was spinning and it wasn't just the caffeine sinus-irrigation that was making me light headed. 'It's a lot to take in. How old are you, exactly?'

'I'm 20.' He stood, unconsciously smoothing down his shirt and drawing my attention to his taut abs. 'Are you ready to go out on the prowl?'

'The what?'

'Hunting down a dress, right? Arjie told me that I'm on the job until you're suited. It's like a quest, innit?'

I grabbed my bag. I was starting to think I'd walked on to a Bollywood film set but who cared! Krishna was gorgeous and I could see that it was going to be very difficult to find the right dress – it could take all day!

From not too far away I could hear music, Indian wedding music, mixed with loud laughter. For a moment I tensed up, then the door opened again and Krishna reappeared in his wedding kurta of purple and gold. He walked towards me, grinning, and put his right hand on my carefully barbered mound. My legs slid apart as if he'd pressed the "open" button.

'Now?' I asked, with considerably more pleading than I'd expected in my tone.

His grin grew bigger. 'Not a hope, Meli. The party will be going on for hours yet, there's no rush.' But his hand slipped down and found the soft wet flesh that I pushed up into his touch before he laughed and pulled away before returning to his teasing game.

I began to thrash from side to side, unable to bear the tension of not coming any longer. Krishna buried his face in my neck and began to kiss me, hot and hard, his teeth gnawing on the tendons in a way that would have made my legs weak if they weren't already totally liquid. If my hands had been free I would have grabbed his hard-on right then, certain that he wouldn't have been able to resist a good squeeze of his glans, but I was helpless, deliciously unable to do anything but accept what he was willing to offer and endure what he was taking pleasure in handing out. Even Hilad had never pushed me to this point, in fact I hadn't known there was a point this far along the joined path of pain and pleasure, and I wondered what else I might discover.

Krishna spoke, but his words were muffled by my hair and the position he was in.

'What?' I tried to turn my head so I could hear him.

'Gotta go again Meli. Got to do my duty as an uncle of the groom. Back soon ...' His fingers trailed down my body and then rose to straighten his hair. 'Do I look decent?'

He stuck his hip out and pouted, and I was again amazed at how little machismo Indian guys had, and how absolutely wonderful it was that they were able to enjoy their feminine side so completely. Mind you, I would have been happier if he'd enjoyed my feminine side a bit more thoroughly – I was aching to come!

Krishna walked to the door, then turned round and came back to me, putting one knee on the bed and sliding two fingers straight into me. He must have known what was going to happen because even before I realised myself that I was about to head into screaming orgasm, his other hand came down gently but very firmly over my mouth and I screamed into his fingers as my whole body, from my heels to my shoulders, rose from the bed in a huge curve that was simply focused on getting as much of his hand inside me as possible. It didn't build, it just arrived, like a fast car, the way that guys always say they come but I never had, it was like slamming into a brick wall of pleasure and being knocked out by total physical joy. I swear the whole world went velvet black.

Then, while I was shuddering and moaning with the

aftershock of complete orgasm, Krishna bent, kissed me, slipping his tongue into my mouth and out again, and left once more.

I let my body relax, wondering if Krishna smelt of me and sex, and whether Hilad would recognise the fragrance. I'd seen the woman who was destined to become his wife – she was tiny and silent and seemed completely fazed by the wedding. I was pretty boggled by it myself – I'd had no idea that Hilad was quite so "fusion", and Vidya turned out to be a total head-case in the best possible way. The do was a blend of Posh and Becks meets traditional Hindu. Vidya was wearing a red and gold ball gown, Hilad sported a traditional kurta with an embroidered waistcoat over the top, bearing an orchid buttonhole. The groomsmen wore kurtas and top hats and the bridesmaids wore saris and killer heels. It was the most amazing mixture of cultures and styles and somehow they were managing to pull it all off.

I'd really been enjoying the party, not least because Hilad obviously hadn't expected to see me. My lavender silk dress toned brilliantly with Krishna's kurta and I saw Hilad scowl as he worked out that Krishna and I knew each other. Revenge would have been sweet, if I'd even cared, but I didn't. I was so past caring that I barely noticed his bad temper.

Finding the dress had been fun, mainly because Krishna seemed to want to show me the whole of Birmingham before we got down to shopping. We began by drinking lassi in a little Indian café where everybody seemed to be his relative.

'So, apart from being Arjun's uncle, and the youngest taxi-driver in Brum, what else should I know about you?' I couldn't believe I was flirting with him, OK, he wasn't exactly a toy-boy – 20 to my 27 wasn't that much of a stretch, but I'd never been interested in men younger than myself. But I couldn't help it; he seemed to enjoy life so much that it was infectious.

He became serious for a second. 'OK. I have five brothers and six sisters. My mother thinks I'm a miracle because she was fifty-one when I was born. I've been spoilt all my life, I have the IQ of a genius and I'm named for the love-god. That's all you need to know.'

'The love-god?' If I was flirting, he was taking it to the next level.

'Lord Krishna is said to have had 16,000 concubines. That's who I'm named for.'

Phew! This young man certainly wasn't lacking in confidence. I found myself wiping my mouth extra-carefully so I didn't end up with a lassi-moustache for the rest of the day. Whether I was hoping he would kiss me or not, I preferred not to consider, but I knew that if he did, I wasn't going to complain.

We went to his sister's sari shop, his sister-in-law's boutique, one brother's supermarket to pick up groceries, another brother's house to drop them off – it was a web of interrelationships where everybody welcomed Krishna when he arrived and begged him to stay when it was time to leave. He was right, he was spoilt. On the other hand though, he was always smiling and funny, and clearly adored his brothers and sisters as much as they did him.

We finished the day in a tiny shop I hadn't even known existed, run by a sister of one of Krishna's sisters-in-law. I couldn't even work out the relationships and no longer cared, I was having a great time. They sold one-off dresses, many of them produced by fashion students at the end of their courses for the final show. Most of the stuff was too whacky for me, but one dress, lavender silk with a handkerchief hem, was perfect.

I turned my head; I could see it now, crumpled on the floor beside the bed. I looked up, straining my neck to see the purple silk scarf that Krishna had handed me at the end of our trip. 'This is for you,' he'd said. 'I want you to wear it to the wedding.'

I hadn't been wrong to read something significant into that.

Straight after Arjun and Vidya walked around the ceremonial fire four times, with Vidya giggling like crazy the whole way, Krishna took my arm and led me to a bedroom off the main wedding suite.

'You know it's good luck to make love during a wedding, don't you, Meli?' He grinned at me and I grinned back as he lifted the scarf from my shoulders and slid the dress down my arms. Then, before I fully realised what was going on, he'd knotted the scarf around my wrists and bent to slide his arms beneath my shoulders and knees, carrying me the two steps to the bed, before kneeling in front of me and taking a roll of bondage tape from the pocket of his kurta.

'And you know that Indian weddings can last for days, don't you, Meli?' His eyes were very dark and hot, and I nodded, struck silent by the intensity of the moment. There was still fun, but now there was something stronger and darker in the way he looked at me.

So I let him bind my breasts and tie me to the bed. I lay there, and felt my heart thudding as if somebody was beating a drum far away. Krishna bent over me, his lips brushing my forehead, 'I have to go and make sure my nephew gets married properly. But I'll be back soon, Meli, to take care of you.'

I lay there, hearing the distant music and laughter, wondering, but only idly, if Hilad and his "new lady" were having a good time. I certainly was!

The door opened again. Krisha stood before me, but this time, instead of walking to the bed he stopped and pulled off his kurta, revealing those muscular abs that I'd been so aware of the day he took me shopping.

'Now,' he said, 'the wedding can do without me. But I

can't do without you any more.'

He walked over and knelt on the bed, pulling a handful of condoms from his pocket. I watched as he rolled it onto his cock, giving the job a level of care and attention that made me hotter than ever. Then he stroked my belly and thighs, watching my face as I arched and twisted under his hands, wanting him, until eventually he grinned again, and lowered himself, sliding himself inside me with silky ease.

I felt the scream building again, as his length filled me and we moved against each other without friction. Krishna rose, pressing his mouth over mine, so that my cries were muffled by his soft lips. 'You scream, Meli,' he whispered, when the orgasm was over. 'You yell and scream as much as you like, we've got all night.'

I bucked my hips so that he went even deeper. 'Trust me, Krishna,' I muttered between gasps of pleasure. 'I'll make you scream with pleasure too, before this night's over.'

And I looked up into his dark eyes and knew that I'd said exactly what he wanted to hear.

The Clearing
by Chris Ross

For Lucy, the temptation of an afternoon in the sun was just too much, so she grabbed a blanket, her iPod and some sun-oil and headed for the forest.

Joining the hidden path, she wound her way through the trees for about ten minutes, before leaving the path towards the clearing she knew so well. She soon arrived at the spot – a space roughly 50 metres square, surrounded by low trees and bushes and totally quiet and private.

She laid out her blanket on the soft grass, set out her iPod and removed her clothes, folding them for a pillow. Should I remove my panties? she wondered. She so loved to be naked in the sun. Looking around and listening, all she could make out was the sound of the birds, so she stripped her panties off too. The hot sun on her skin was making her slightly horny, as it always did.

Taking the oil, she put some into her hands and began to smooth it over her breasts, loving the sensations as she ran her hands over her sensitive nipples. Concentrating on one with each hand, she squeezed and gently tugged, feeling the tingling as they expanded and hardened under her fingers.

Lucy had always had sensitive nipples, but they were so often left neglected – something she could correct when she was by herself! She rubbed her fingers over them, slick with oil and warmed by the sun. She was in danger of getting carried away. Pulling her thoughts back, she moved on to her arms and shoulders, then on down towards her belly.

Oiling her body always had an unfortunate effect on her. She moved down to oil her legs, but as she came up to her thighs she felt a familiar tingling sensation within her as her pussy began to moisten.

She looked around again. The clearing was empty as it usually was at this time; a gentle breeze blew across her skin and the sun blazed down. Who could it hurt? She was alone, wasn't she? She lay on her back, the soft grass beneath the blanket making a wonderful bed. As she parted her legs the warm sun on her pussy made her tremble slightly, but it was a wonderful sensation. She moved her hands across her inner thighs and gently brushed her outer lips with her fingertips. She slipped one inside and was not surprised to find how wet she was already.

Opening her legs wider, she slipped in a second finger, curling them inwards and upwards as she felt for her magic spot. A wave of pleasure coursed through her body as she found it and pressed gently, moving her fingertips rhythmically from side to side. She arched her back – something told her this wasn't going to take long.

Rubbing harder she felt the sensations begin, rippling up through her body as she caught her breath. She rubbed harder as the feelings grew more intense, her legs began to shake, her belly tightening, until suddenly she gasped, her fingers frozen, unable to move from the spot. She increased the pressure to prolong the sensation and held her breath.

As the orgasm subsided, she panted as she slowly removed her fingers and massaged them gently over her quivering pussy as she relaxed back onto the blanket exhausted. Putting on her earphones, she turned on her favourite music and began to doze.

Lucy realised she must have fallen asleep for some time, as the sun was now on the side of her face. She opened her eyes and was shocked to discover she was no longer alone! She quickly shut them again, but she didn't dare to move. Obviously, while she had slept someone had found the clearing and decided to stay. Carefully opening one eye again, she found herself looking at a man. He was wearing only a pair of loose shorts and he was sitting on a tree-stump with a small rucksack at his feet.

He was looking directly at her – and she remembered she was still completely naked. She knew he hadn't noticed she had woken up, because it wasn't her face he was looking at!

Still pretending to be asleep, she let herself sigh gently and moved a little which allowed her legs to part. The man quickly turned away but then let his gaze drift back, his hand moving to adjust the front of his shorts. She knew he must be finding this quite arousing – it was having the same effect on her.

Still feigning sleep, she moved again, and angled her body towards him. She wanted to allow him a better view. This time he didn't turn away. Through half-closed eyes, Lucy tried to look at him more closely. He was in his late 40s and he looked tall, fit and tanned. He had a full head of slightly greying hair and a light covering of chest hair.

She realised she found this stranger quite attractive and knew she wanted him to watch her – it was most definitely turning her on. She sighed again and let her hand drift down between her legs as she watched him swallow hard. She guessed his mouth had gone dry.

Lucy let her fingers slide over her pussy and she gently parted the lips. She was already wet again. She moved her other hand to join the first and opened her pussy to the sun, enjoying the feeling of its warmth on her inner lips, and knowing she was fully exposed. She moved her fingers to her clit and began massaging gently. She began to get lost in the moment, knowing all the time that she was being watched by a handsome stranger. She sighed again – her arousal was making her feel very brave. Not opening her eyes she said aloud, 'Please, won't you join me?' while she continued to play with her pussy and clit, and hoped she hadn't frightened him away.

She waited – enjoying the feeling of her fingers on her soft flesh.

She had heard nothing, but suddenly she felt a gentle kiss on her breast. She gasped, but knew he had taken up her generous offer. With his soft tongue he circled her nipple, taking it into his mouth as it hardened to his touch.

Oh, how she loved a man who gave her breasts the attention they craved. His hand found her belly and his fingertips lightly played on her skin. Lucy shivered, expectantly. His fingers moved further down to join her own, as he nibbled slightly on her now erect nipple causing that wonderful feeling of pleasure and pain. She felt a trickle of wetness escape her pussy and run slowly down between her bum cheeks.

Soon his kisses were moving down her front, pausing to tease her belly-button before continuing further. Without warning, his tongue was on her clitoris and in automatic response she lifted her hips towards him. His tongue licked and teased and probed, as his hands came up to roughly massage her breasts and engorged nipples. And then, abruptly, he was gone.

For a moment she felt lost and confused, and feared to open her eyes. Then she sensed him again as he kneeled astride her head. His body now blocked the sun as he leaned forward to move her hands away from her pussy, his tongue running down her belly again before he buried his face between her legs. She knew exactly what she had to do.

She moved her hands up until she felt his thighs, then she slid them further upwards and inwards to find his erect penis hovering above her face. She opened her eyes to get a good look at his cock. She liked to see what she was going to get, so she admired the large organ that she now held in her hands.

She touched it with her tongue and felt his involuntary twitch. She circled her fingers around it, enjoying the stiffness she knew she had caused. Tilting her head back, she drew it down further towards her mouth and ran her tongue around the rim. Experience told her this could drive men wild, but somehow she felt that wouldn't be necessary in this case! But it was still fun.

She licked her way up to the end and let her lips close around the engorged head and began pulling it further into her. She slowly eased it back out again, all the time playing her tongue around it, until she felt his own tongue once more find her clitoris. At the same time he slid one of his fingers gently and slowly into her now soaking pussy.

She lifted her head, taking all of his impressive cock into her mouth until he nudged the back of her throat. Then she moved back again, intent on teasing him some more. Her hand gently squeezed his balls as she clamped her lips harder around his shaft, sliding him in and out. Concentrating then on the rim around the head of his penis she licked and sucked for all she was worth.

Meanwhile, he started to make gentle movements in time with her own – penetrating her mouth, all the time letting his fingers and tongue tease her now aching pussy. Then his finger found her magic spot, rubbing firmly while his tongue flicked over her pouting clitoris. My God, she thought, how much more of this can I take?

As if in answer, she started to get the familiar feeling as her pussy began to throb and she knew she wouldn't hold out much longer. At that same moment, she felt him start to thrust harder at her mouth and knew his own moment had almost arrived.

Then she felt the first wave of her own orgasm grow. She thrust her hips off the ground and hard against his fingers, then threw back her head as the sensation tore through her. A burst of fluid exploded from her pussy as she experienced her first ever ejaculation. She slowly lowered her head and shoulders while she gasped for breath – and realised suddenly he was no longer on top of her.

Where did he go? thought Lucy and, more to the point,

how does he *do* that?

She found out where he'd gone when she felt a pressure between her legs, gently forcing them apart and she understood there was more to come. He placed his hands under her bum, and raised her hips up towards him. He bent forward, running his tongue over her still-quivering pussy, darting it in and out of her hot pussy, before finally closing his lips around her tender clitoris and sucking gently.

Lucy moved her hands onto her breasts to tease her own nipples, rubbing and pulling, adding to the pleasure she was already feeling further down. Lowering her once more to the ground he inserted one, then two fingers into her, meeting almost no resistance – all the time massaging her clitoris with his tongue. He drew his fingers back, but then, as he pushed into her again, she felt her pussy being stretched a little.

Once more he withdrew and this time as he came back into her she felt the stretch rather more. She moaned softly and moved herself on his fingers, knowing that by now he must have all four inside her. Her pussy was now stretched to accommodate them, as she put her head back and sighed again at this new and unexpected sensation.

He continued to slide his fingers in and out, each time opening her a little wider, going a little deeper. She took a deep breath, arched her back, and tried to force herself onto him. But he followed her movements, teasing her and causing her to moan in frustration. Now she began to feel a greater pressure. Surely not? she thought, Surely this can't be happening?

But she could no longer help herself. Her passion had now taken over and she began to feel the adrenaline rush. She forced her legs wider apart as she drew her knees up, anticipating what was to happen, losing herself in the feeling of being stretched wider and wider, knowing that she was now gaping open for his inspection.

When it came, it took her breath away. She gasped as she

26

took his whole hand into her. The sensation was something she could never have imagined in her wildest dreams. It was an intense pressure inside her that she had never experienced before.

She orgasmed instantly, her whole body shaking uncontrollably, her head spinning as she grabbed his wrist with one hand and forced herself onto him. With her other hand, her fingers found her clit and she rubbed it hard and fast. He slowly and carefully drew his hand out, before pushing it back in again and again, while her fingers were a blur on her clit. She squirmed and writhed against him, and then she threw her head back as the second orgasm exploded through her body. For a while she couldn't breath. Then, with a huge gasp, she sank back into the blanket as he gently eased his hand out of her – kissing, licking and caressing her now gaping pussy.

Relaxing in the aftermath of this amazing new experience, she ran her fingers through his hair while he continued to lick and kiss between her legs and over her belly. Slowly he moved away a little, but instead of getting up, he rolled her onto her front and, putting some oil onto his hands, he began to massage her back. He was good at it too, easing her shoulders and applying a little pressure as he ran his thumbs down her spine. She began to relax with the combination of the heat and his touch.

Inevitably, his hands began to stray lower as he gently oiled her bum. She had always been proud of her curves, and he certainly seemed to appreciate them too. At first gently, then a little more forcefully, his thumbs strayed down into the crack between her cheeks, teasing her. Feeling relaxed and warm, she enjoyed the sensation as she had rarely received a massage, and certainly never in such surroundings.

Without even thinking, she raised her hips up towards him. In response, he knelt between her legs and, using her own juices, massaged her bum, straying between her legs

27

and teasing her anus. She felt the unexpected tingle of yet another new sensation. He continued with the massage, but more and more his fingers teased her delicately. She reached back behind her to return the favour, and was pleasantly surprised to discover that his cock had recovered its former glory and was already standing to attention.

He eased closer and she let her fingers encircle it, rubbing slowly up and down. As she did so, she felt his fingertip push gently into her arse, causing the tingle to increase in intensity. Taking the lead this time, she eased her hips towards him, slowly drawing his cock towards her.

She felt him hesitate, and heard the rustle of a packet and realised what he was doing, but the waiting only made her more eager. She tilted her hips even more and, placing his cock in position, she guided him gently into her waiting pussy. In response he moved his finger further into her arse, causing her muscles to tense involuntarily, but she forced herself to relax. Today was a day for new experiences and she was keen to try everything.

She began to rock rhythmically against his cock and he matched the movements, withdrawing fully, before pushing in again, his hips hard up against her. She could feel the full length of him inside her as he continued to tease her other entrance. As his thrusts became more intense, she moved her own fingers back to her clit and began to rub. She forced her hips back harder with each thrust and she felt him add a second finger to the penetration of her arse. A little ripple of pleasure and excitement ran through her.

Never before had she felt the sensation of two penetrations at the same time. The feeling was surprisingly intense. She rubbed her clit harder as his thrusts became faster, his cock filling her as his fingers now began to thrust in and out too. All three sensations combined together, tipping her over the edge into an intense orgasm that made her cry out. Burying her face in the blanket, she clamped around his cock, as she felt his orgasm deep within her. He

28

stayed still for only a few moments, panting slightly before withdrawing and slowly backing away.

She lowered herself down to the blanket utterly sated, buried her face in her clothes and, with the heat and exhaustion, she drifted off to sleep.

On waking, after what she was sure were only a few minutes, she found she was again alone in the clearing. She looked around, sure he must be there somewhere, but could see no sign, although her gently throbbing pussy, confirmed it had certainly been no dream. As she stood up and looked towards where she had first seen him, she saw something on the tree stump where he had been sitting.

Dressing quickly and collecting her things, she walked across to it. On the stump she found a single red rose of the most exquisite shape and colour. Beside it lay a small card, on which was simply written, To my beautiful forest angel, thank you! A small tear escaped her eye as she tried to remember the last time somebody had called her beautiful.

Though she returned to the clearing many times that summer, undressing and waiting, dozing on her blanket, the stranger never returned. But for ever in her dreams in that place, would come the amazing sensations of that incredible day. And the knowledge that somebody thought she was beautiful, gave her a new-found confidence to go out and face the world.

Libertines
by Cyanne

The artist's eyes burned into me as he painted, looking scantly at the canvas, but searing over my body and face, drinking in every detail.

'*Cherie,* your energy is taking over me. Of all the models in Montmartre you are the most beautiful: the body of a whore with the eyes of a virgin.'

My cheeks reddened at his words. I was not a virgin, but near enough. Jacques had clumsily taken my virginity and grunted away on top of me every night thereafter until I took my savings and left for Paris, with all its vices and promises.

His brush scratched at the canvas and globs of marbled gouache splattered the worn carpet, threadbare where his artistic temperament paced him sleeplessly up and down. A semi-conscious young girl on the chaise longue moaned with pleasure as a well-dressed man's hand disappeared under her skirts. They called it Art Nouveau, and I was desperate to be a part of it.

'I must paint you without the shackles of that peasanty dress, *Cherie,* I cannot bear it any longer. Please strip it away.'

I blushed. The model on the couch stirred from her arousal and absinthe-induced haze to witness my embarrassment. She laughed as I refused to take off my dress and untangled herself from the clutches of her momentary beau to walk over to me on the pedestal.

'Such a pretty *décolletage',* she slurred as she pushed

my dress down over my shoulders. Her hands roamed my chest and I was frozen in my standing pose, half with fright, half with an unexpected pleasure at her drunken touch.

'Yet such a horrible dress!' And with a swift tug my dress was around my waist and my breasts were exposed to the room. The man on the couch lit a cigarette and stared lecherously and the artist made a sound of approval. Tears rose in my eyes but I could not deny the frisson of delight that came along with the scorch of humiliation. The artist flung the clothed painting from his easel and began sketching me topless.

The man on the sofa rang the bell and the butler appeared almost instantly.

'More absinthe, *Monsieur*?'

'No, we have enough here. I just thought you deserved to see this fine young woman in a state of undress. Look at those perky young breasts; have you ever seen anything so beautiful?'

The shame overcame me and I made to cover myself, but the artist scolded me and I resumed my position, the wetness between my legs just becoming noticeable.

As darkness fell over Paris the artist asked me to walk with him. He said he had lots of money and would show me the sights. We wove down streets where hustlers played card tricks on the unsuspecting, and whores plied their wares out of dimly lit doorways, their bosoms bursting out and their rouge heavy. Up and up we walked, to the Basilica of Sacre Coeur.

'From here, you can see all of Paris.'

I leaned on the wall and looked out over the glittering lights of the city. She suited the night; you could smell the expectation in the air. The new century was just around the corner and the world was changing.

The artist came up behind me and I could feel his arousal even through the layers of clothing that separated us.

'You stirred something in me today. I have never

painted so intensely. If it is your wish, you will live with me, as my muse.'

His hands rose up the backs of my legs, making me tingle. My skirts fell forward onto the wall and the evening breeze made tiny bumps rise on my legs. The artist caressed my bottom and my sex grew wet and ready. He deftly untied the straps of my undergarments and they fell to the ground – the grounds of a church no less! I panicked and struggled but he held me facing away from him, my bare bottom pressed against his trousers and my sex naked in the night air.

'Freedom, *Chérie*. We are *les libertines*. We can do whatever we please.'

With that he was on his knees, his face buried between my legs like an animal, pressing my legs wider. His tongue was warm and his curls tickled the inside of my thighs. He licked me up and down hungrily, gripping handfuls of flesh at my hips. The thought of being caught brought on my climax, a stronger and more devastating orgasm than I had ever experienced. I flooded his face and struggled and failed to keep my mouth shut and avoid the curious glances from those promenading below.

He insisted I left my undergarments where they lay, kicking them across the ground. He said women in the city were starting to wear stockings held up by belts and clips, and that he would take me shopping for this new fashion soon.

We walked arm in arm to the Moulin Rouge, where crowds bustled outside. A dangerous-looking man in an expensive frock coat and silk neck tie ushered us towards him. The artist introduced us and we went under the infamous windmill into the iniquitous salon. Women stared at the man as he passed, whispering amongst themselves, as a serving girl showed us to a table right at the front. I stared aghast as a curvaceous blonde woman lifted her skirts higher and higher to the screams of the assembly, revealing her scant undergarments and the red heart embroidered thereon.

The man leaned close to me. 'La Goulue,' he whispered gruffly, making me jump as a hint of stubble grazed my cheek and a scent of masculinity tugged at my already engorged arousal.

'She's the queen of Moulin Rouge. Vulgar really, but you ...' His hand strayed up my leg, discarding my layers of skirts easily. 'You have real class.'

He turned to the artist.

'You must let me sample your new delicacy,' he said, his hand casually resting on the inside of my knee. I was painfully aware of my lack of underwear, but responded to his touch in spite of myself, seduced by the dim smoky room charged with sexual energy.

The artist locked gazes with me.

'Be my guest.'

The man's hand rose higher, finding my inner thighs locked together with guilt and shame, but easily opening them with kisses to my throat and collar bones. His teeth bit down on my neck, my mouth opened and I sunk into his embrace, aware of the artist's eyes on me as his sipped his Absinthe. The man's finger strayed higher and persuaded my legs to part, finding me soaking wet. One finger dipped inside me then retreated, teasing, making me push my hips forward to meet him. His fingers circled my clit making me cry out loud. I grabbed a glass of wine from the table and muffled as much of my flushing face as I could with it. The artist moved his chair closer and they both bit on my neck. The artist ran his hands across my breasts and pulled down the front of my gown, exposing a glimpse of nipple. A couple of people stared but most were too embroiled in their own excesses to notice or care.

The artist's hand rode under my clothes, pushing my skirts up above the knee and his fingers joined the man's, bumping their knuckles against each other 'til I didn't know whose fingers were inside me. I climaxed wetly, thrashing in my seat, trying to keep the ecstasy off my face.

We drank, there was dancing, I was intoxicated not just by the liquor but the smoke and the giddiness. As we stood to leave I stumbled, drunk, and four strong arms caught me.

A tiny man, barely the size of a child sidled up to us and I startled, unsure if I was having a green-fairy-induced hallucination. He handed me a rolled up scroll of paper and limped off. My companions laughed at my bemusement.

'That's Henri de Toulouse Lautrec,' said the artist. 'An impressionist of some talent, but a cripple and a terrible drunkard.'

'But,' the man confided with a wink, 'all the girls say he has a massive cock.'

I giggled – it just kept getting weirder – and unfurled the scroll. Taken aback does not begin to describe the feeling of seeing myself, hastily but accurately rendered in pastel, my skirts hitched up above the knee and two men's hands between my legs!

By the time we got back to the artist's apartment it was filled with people, draped all over the furniture and each other, the smell of sex in the air. The artist was drunk and loud.

'I must paint!' he announced to no one in particular, then addressed me, '*Chérie* take the pedestal. I want to feast on art tonight!'

I stumbled up onto the small platform and tried to pose through my drunken haze.

'No, no, no! Undress!' he shouted.

The people started to take notice and catcall for me to strip. Emboldened by the drink and the fact that I had posed topless earlier that day, I pulled down the front of my dress, freeing my breasts. The sudden power over the men in the room was glorious, and I stuck out my chest to win even more of their admiration.

'All the way off, I'm in the mood for sketching you, not

a bunch of fabric.'

I hardly knew who I was any more. The simple country girl in me blushed at exposing a mere shoulder, and I thought of her as I pulled my dress over my hips, leaving just a scant petticoat. I was naked underneath and I could tell by the stares that my pubic hair was showing through. I revelled in the feeling. I could tell I was turning the whole room on. People had their hands on each other, other bare breasts began to appear in darker corners, heads were thrown back to meet voracious kisses.

A girl joined me on the pedestal, freeing her blonde hair from its clasp as she jumped up. Her breasts were already bursting from the front of her dress and in no time she was free of its constraints, stripped down to a pair of short knickers and some of the black wool stockings the artist had told me about. The black stockings looked stunning against her pale skin and she pulled me close into a pose, eyes locked on the artist as he scribbled and scrawled.

The men in the room were getting more and more excited, and those that didn't have their own woman to fondle drew nearer and nearer to us. Hands began to pull at my petticoat, first lightly, then, when my protests were perfunctory and laughing, a little harder, baring a little more of me.

A couple on the sofa were locked into a deep kiss when the man broke away, pulled open the girl's legs and buried his face between them. She pulled at the back of his head, not caring that other men were shuffling closer and closer to look at her most private parts.

The girl got on her knees in front of me, her breath warm on my thighs, and a man came up behind her and tugged her panties down, baring her beautiful pussy. Men slapped her arse and grabbed her breasts and she buried her face against me in pleasure. With the help of a mystery man behind me she pulled down my petticoat and I was naked on the stage, hands coming from all angles to touch me. She

36

pushed my legs apart and her tongue was on my pussy, so much softer and gentler than a man's. The men called out to encourage us and I stood awkwardly, legs wide with nothing to hold on to, eyes wide with pleasure and disbelief at the scene in the room.

The artist frowned in concentration, sketching furiously as he attempted to render the bacchanalian scene.

Hands supported me to the floor as my knees got weaker and weaker. The girl was on her knees licking me with a small crowd of men behind her sipping drinks and rubbing themselves through their trousers as they looked at her bare sex presented up to them. Occasionally she moaned into me, her breath hot, as one of them reached forward and tested her with a finger, sucking it appreciatively afterwards, their hard cocks pushing at their clothing.

A man approached with the Absinthe bottle, dripping it into my open mouth. The heady scent of opium hung in the air, no one was in their right mind, but I briefly thought to myself, these are just things everyone wished they could do sober, but did not dare.

The chilly green liquid spilled down my sides as the man poured it across my chest, leaning in to lick it off, and quickly being joined by others, eager to get even more intoxicated, and drink in my body in the process. Lips sucked my nipples and thighs and tongues trailed over my stomach and sides, tickling me into a frenzy. The girl slipped her fingers inside me and I climaxed noisily, writhing in the spilt drink and held by multiple hands.

The artist approached and embraced me, leading me to his easel, where we talked and watched as the room fucked and stroked and licked, drinking and smoking and feeling the joy of being alive. Unselfconsciously naked, I embraced him as he sketched, and listened to his stories of Paris. He held me, touched me, but would not make love to me, despite my unladylike pleas.

As the sun rose, the revellers slept where they fell, and

37

the artist and I left the crazy scene and took coffee in the square. He took me shopping as promised, and bought me the fashionable underwear he had mentioned. I felt like a harlot in the most delicious way and told him so.

'But would you like to feel like a harlot for real, *Chérie?*'

I'd always been fascinated with the ladies of the night, their red lights, their immodest clothing, their whispered sorority, their power and irreplaceable social function. I envisaged a role play scene, where I would dress up for him, he would pretend to pay me a nominal fee, and I would finally get to feel him inside me after stopping short the night before. I replied that I would like that very much.

How I found myself standing in the shadows of late-night Montmartre, pulling a shawl around my shoulders while trying to show off enough to compete with the gloriously overstated femininity all around me, I wasn't quite sure. The artist said he would watch from a café-bar over the street, and that my experience would be an inspiration. I could just make out his form behind the steamed up window, ordering a Ricard, getting out his sketchbooks and charcoal. The women eyed me with suspicion – they all seemed to know each other – and bustled past me as they approached the furtive men.

A tall man approached, walking directly towards me. After the warmth and openness of the artists, his brusque, '*Combien?*' jarred. I stumbled to reply. Was I really going to do this? As he followed me up the narrow stairs of the grubby and clandestine *pension* I moved as I had seen the women move, accentuating my hips and backside, slatternly and practised. I wasn't, of course, and inwardly I was cowering as the door closed behind him and I sat down on the bed.

He handed me the money, no nominal sum, and told me to undress. He reclined and watched, never meeting my eyes, staring, hungry at my body as I revealed it. Topless, stripped down to the little panties and black stockings the artist had bought for me, he told me to get on all fours. He pushed my head down, pulled my underwear to the side, and entered me roughly from behind, pulling my legs apart as he did. Grunting, he thrust into me harder and harder. My body responded to the man taking control and I cried out. He smelt of clean sweat and felt firm and strong, easily controlling me. His fingers twined into my hair and as he lifted my head back I caught sight of myself in the mirror, hair curling out of control, perspiration around my forehead and breasts bare, a stranger using me, fucking me from behind, his back arching as he pushed into me, his thrusts becoming more staccato as he neared his climax. For money, no less. Money I didn't even need. For art. The woman in the mirror looked sexy, dirty, alive. What would Jacques say?

I told the artist all about it, lying naked on the chaise-longue, drinking Absinthe. He questioned me intricately; how big was the man? How did I feel? The money lay on the table, he said I should spend it on a dress, and stayed up all night painting one of the sketches he'd done of me standing under the streetlamp. He called it *The Whore of Montmartre*, and hung it on the parlour wall in his apartment – he said he would never sell it.

As we talked I attempted to entice him. I let my legs fall apart, over-emphasising intoxication, pushing myself on him. He touched me, rubbing and caressing so expertly that I was pliant in his hands. Unselfconsciously naked, I writhed on the sofa, his fingers deep inside me, opening my legs wide and throwing my head back, certain that he would be overcome with lust and fuck me, as I so ached for him. I was dizzy with arousal, when he leapt up and walked to the easel, his hardness straining against his trousers as he walked.

I made a sound of protest, and he suggested that I carry

on, while he painted me. Even after the debauchery of the last few days, touching myself in front of him piqued a tiny bit of embarrassment in me. Something women weren't even supposed to admit to, let alone make a performance of. I let my hands stray over my breasts and stomach, pausing – was I nervous or teasing? I didn't even know myself! – before pressing my cunt open and lightly touching myself. My fingers felt small and soft after his, but I knew exactly what to do. One leg I threw over the back of the chaise longue, the other foot was on the floor. I begged him to fuck me. He said he never would, that I was his inspiration, that he was a spectator and a journalist of my sexual development, not a part of it. I was a project, a painting, an *objet d'art*.

I was coming close, the exposure of my pertinent nakedness joining the frustration at him rebuffing my advances. The butler cleared his throat. How long he had been standing in the doorway I had no idea. He was more than accustomed to seeing naked people sprawled over the furniture, but I wasn't quite accustomed to being one of them, and I panicked a little. The artist told me not to move, that I had to hold the pose. I lay back, opening my legs wide as they were before.

'How wet is she?' the artist asked the butler.

He walked towards me, unhurriedly. I had never felt more deliciously exposed. He ran his finger between my legs.

'She's soaking wet, *monsieur.*'

'I just need a couple of minutes, keep her there, I need the tension to come across'.

'Of course, *monsieur.*'

The butler put his tray on the table, and bent to his knees. He licked me softly, his tongue imploring my pussy, his touch gentler and less personal that the artist. I started to build towards a climax, and pulled the butler's head closer. He moved away, and stood up. I moaned in anguish, and

40

went to touch myself again.

'No, *mademoiselle,*' he said, and moved my hand away.

The artist scribbled away in the background, and I writhed in frustration, a wet patch forming on the chaise longue. I begged the butler with my eyes and he smiled. My breathing was deep, all my consciousness between my legs, naked and aroused with two fully clothed men regarding me in a composed manner. I was full of raw energy, flushed and wet, but their attentions were deliberate and controlled. The artist's words ran through my head: an *objet d'art* ... The butler disturbed my repetitive thoughts with a hand on my breast, circling the nipple, making me gasp as the tingling in my chest found its way lower. He chased it with his hand, touching my clit so lightly that I screamed for more. People began to trickle into the room, regarding me with lust, interest, boredom, indifference. Everyone had a clear view between my legs and the butler's hand, but I couldn't stop. They drank and smoked and conversed, and I got hotter and wetter.

He pulled away again and I sobbed. I caught the artist's eye through a sweaty tendril of hair, and he smiled a loving smile, his hand never leaving the canvas. Another man joined the butler by the couch, discussing my physical merits positively, but always in the third person.

Occasionally the butler broke off conversing with the man and licked and stroked me, briefly, expertly, but never enough, keeping me on the cusp of climax until my vision was blurred and I was moaning and pleading shamelessly for more. The other man casually touched my nipples, my lips, and my cunt, sizing me up and playing with my extreme arousal for his own entertainment and that of the assembled artists and models. It felt like hours 'til the artist announced he was finished, and turned the canvas for us to see.

My hair was rendered with black streaks, and impressionistic daubs and dashes of red and pink were all around me, catching movement and moments. Between my legs was indecently bright pink, my mouth open and eyes closed.

The butler lifted me up, naked and drenched, and announced that I was available. A handsome and well-built man sat beside me on the chaise and freed his hard cock from his trousers. He smelt strong, masculine. Hands lifted me, and I sank onto him. Mouths kissed mine, hands grabbed at my breasts. Strangers and friends lifted me up and down, sliding my pussy over the man's cock. I was out of control; I rubbed my soaking wet pussy in front of everyone, to sounds of approval from the men. I came hard in their collective arms. I flopped down on the chaise, but the man wasn't left bereft, another girl was waiting to take my place, and I disentangled myself from the increasing orgy.

The artist was standing back, watching. I hardly even realised I was naked any more. It was becoming normal. I asked him again why he watched so much and didn't join in. He said his pleasure was in the gaze. He led me to the balcony, wrapping a silky shawl around me as we walked, his hand in the small of my back in a way that was both gentlemanly and familiar. He spoke seriously, held me, and asked me to stay. He said I could fuck men for money, and he would paint me every day, that there would be more men and women than I could imagine, and wine, and Paris. My life less than a week ago wasn't even in the same world, and of course I said *oui*.

One Night Only
by Alex Severn

Funny, but I didn't fancy her at all to begin with. When I first started at the office, I mean. There were better-looking women there, certainly more outgoing, more flirty, more fun to be with.

I guess it was a slow burn kind of thing with Eva.

We ended up sitting next to each other on a couple of training events and somehow I started to think about her, well about us together really. I started to imagine being with her for the night, began to find excuses for walking past her desk, for stopping to talk to her. She was a bit severe, serious maybe, but that just seemed to make her more interesting. Eva was hopeless at flirting; at least she was with me! Some of the other girls could tease and coax me into … let's just say they got me good and hard pretty quickly, I had to try to disguise the bulge in my trousers after they had treated me to a few well chosen words.

Eva was a green-eyed blonde with a slim neat figure. She never wore anything sexy, not even in the hot summer days, never showed any cleavage, nobody got treated to any glimpses of thigh. At the Christmas party she was classy and elegant, but again not much flesh on view. When you looked at some of the other women, well … but that was when it hit me really. I didn't want to look at the others, I wanted to be near her, smell her perfume, try to break down the barriers.

So, it was Shelley's 40th birthday night out and we were eating at the Indian, the usual choice. Maybe 15 or 20 of us there, more women than men, which is just how I like it, but I had been praying all day that I could end up sitting with her.

And I got my wish. Her dress was red, long and expensive-looking, her hair was even more immaculate and yes she was a very pretty woman but still she had a feeling of being out of bounds, as if she was an expensive ornament made of glass and you could look but not touch, you know? It was getting late, the food was gone, the plates cleared, the drinks re-ordered. Half of the group had gone home, some were driving, some collected by protective partners, etc. Not all of us were drinkers and a few had scuttled off after the last course anyway. Eva and I were sitting at the very end of the long table, and I suddenly noticed there was a real gap between us and the nearest of the rest of the party. Simon and Louise had gone home by then, Mel, Frankie and Laura were at the bar waiting to be served.

But clearly I wasn't the only one who'd noticed that we weren't going to be overheard because right out of the blue, I mean so totally off the wall, Eva leaned closer to me and whispered, 'So how bad do you want me? What are you prepared to do to get me to yourself?'

I must have shown how shocked and taken by surprise I was because she laughed.

'Come on, Danny, you've been eyeing me up long enough, you think I haven't noticed how hard your cock gets when you talk to me?'

I'm not sure what excited me more here, knowing she'd noticed how much I fancied her or the fact she'd used a word like that. Somehow, it was like hearing the pope telling you to fuck off.

'OK, Eva, I like you, so what are you saying to me?' A hopeless and desperate attempt to be cool with my heart pounding.

God she gave me the wickedest filthiest smile I ever saw.

'Maybe tonight is your lucky night, tonight you get to

enjoy me the way you want to. You know I live alone; you can come back with me. We can be discreet and pretend to go our separate ways , meet later on but ... you need to understand my rules.'

Well I was really hooked now, wasn't I?

'OK, the girls will be back from the bar soon and they'll be able to hear us so you've probably got a minute or so to decide, right? If you come back with me, you agree to do everything I tell you once we're in my flat, and I mean everything, Danny. I take control, you submit totally to me. You will be mine completely, my slave, my man. That's what turns me on. You'll never have had a night like it, I swear it. That's the deal, take it or leave it. And this is the only chance you ever get with me. This is what gets me off, my way ... walk away from this, and you can spend as long as you want wondering what might have been ... You're standing on the edge of a fantasy, the point of no return. Make your choice, Danny boy.'

Something about her words made me shiver, but God I was so turned on. What was this tempting, reserved woman really into? Bondage maybe, a bit of punishment, maybe she needed to be a bad girl so she could get spanked? Maybe she ...

'Now, tell me. They're on their way back. Tonight or never?'

'Yes, yes, I want you tonight.'

The next hour was almost unbearable. Eva had coolly managed to write her address on a napkin and ordered me (well that's how it felt) to make my excuses and leave around 11.30, nice and innocently. My eyes were glued to the top of her dress and I saw, or maybe just imagined, her nipples hardening against the fabric, as if they were trying to reach me. But when she excused herself and went to the ladies I didn't imagine her stumbling against me as I sat there, and making sure her hand brushed against my hard shaft. I was at boiling point and didn't she just know it.

When I knocked on her door and she let me in, I was right on time of course. I guess I was a little disappointed to see she was wearing the same dress but then did I think she would answer the door in stockings and suspenders?

She beckoned me to a small but immaculately tidy living room.

'OK, my rules from now until you leave. Remember you only get this one night with me. You are my property and you take whatever you get, right. You just obey me, and until I say differently, you are not allowed to speak. Break my rules and you go home and this never happened and never will again. You can nod or shake your head, agreed?'

I nodded.

'Right, strip for me; I want to see what I've brought here.'

I mean I was so hard for her, it was a struggle to get my boxers off over my cock but I stood there with my pole jutting towards her.

'Kneel quickly.'

Eva went across to a wall unit and produced a pair of handcuffs and I began to think, OK, bondage is fine for me. Maybe we cuff each other, play a little rough, cool. She moved my right hand behind my back and attached it to my right ankle. Then she did the same to my left side so I was there like a turkey trussed up for Christmas. She smiled.

'Like to see what I've got on offer, darling?'

'Oh yes, I'd like that.'

Boy did I regret that, she strode over and slapped me hard across the face twice, I felt the sting of pain pulse across me.

'I told you not to speak, slave. Do it again without permission and I'll really make you pay, get it?'

I couldn't nod quickly enough. But the smile soon returned and she peeled off the dress to reveal a low cut white lacy bra, very skimpy knickers to match and hold-up stockings. As I held my breath, Eva slipped a hand inside her knickers and began to explore. I groaned and prayed that wouldn't count as speaking but it was so great to see the way she was massaging and stroking even though the fabric stopped me seeing how wet she was getting, I had to imagine her wet pussy lips oozing with her sticky juices ... But then she paused and turned up the intensity of the smile even more.

'Like that do you? Well maybe you can just imagine it for yourself.'

Suddenly she was tying a blindfold around me, good and tight, but I could sense that she was oh-so-close to me still. My cock felt like a billiard cue to me and my balls started pulsing and throbbing ... And I heard her moaning and breathing heavily, my mind was racing, had she pulled her knickers off yet, maybe she was naked now, if I could just see her nipples, I bet they were harder than diamonds ... Then I felt my mouth being prised open and I heard her say

'Now, lick my fingers dry, taste me in your mouth, slave.'

I was so eager to please and I loved the taste of her come in my dry mouth. All too soon she pulled them from me and I was left gasping for more.

'Listen, Danny, everybody at work thinks I'm really straight and boring, I know some of the guys want to fuck me, but most of the girls think I don't bother with men. You know what I love to do? I love to talk real dirty to a man but not when he can see me. I could phone a man, maybe I should get work with one of those phone sex lines but tonight I can watch you as you listen to me, see how far I can take you. Well you can only hear me now, can't you? If you say one word this ends and you go home and think about what you might have missed, I mean it ...

'You know what I love, babe? I love to suck cock, love the taste of a real hard shaft in my mouth. The way it feels when I'm sucking and licking a man really gets me so wet. But I love just as much to see another woman do it for a man, to see a gorgeous girl's lips all over a piece of man meat really drives me wild, you know? And when I watch it I can make myself so wet and open, I'm touching my lips now, Danny, pity you can't see it, isn't it? You really want to fuck me good and hard don't you, Danny, can you imagine how good I look with my legs open just for you? Now I'm on all fours with my arse close to your mouth. Maybe you want to take me that way, pump me from behind. Think of your shaft sliding in and out of my open arse … feels good … yes?'

She stopped talking for a second and my whole body shivered as I felt pressure on the inside of both my thighs, God she must be stroking me with those long slim fingers. Or maybe it was her toes. Abruptly, I felt pressure disappear from my left thigh but intensify on the right. Then she was talking again.

'Feel how close I am to your cock, Danny. And Christ I am so wet for you, my fingers are very busy all over my soaking wet open pussy. Like to lick my sweet pussy would you, slave? Like to rub my clit with your tongue, taste me and drink my honey juices, yes? Well maybe you deserve a treat.'

I felt a push behind my neck and suddenly my mouth was clamped onto her saturated throbbing slit. I was so hot and hard for this amazing woman I wanted to make it the best licking she'd ever taken. The folds and crevices of her pussy seemed to engulf my tongue, I felt her honey juices pouring down my chin and oozing along my mouth. I heard her gasping and moaning and as her noise increased so did the intensity of my eating her out. I changed the angle and speed of my tongue thrusts, lapping and teasing, moving up every few seconds and grazing my teeth against the hard nub of her beautiful clit. I felt as if I was drowning in her come, but then I felt shock waves surge through her pussy, her thighs, and as her muscles tensed she eased herself away from me.

My cock was so rock hard I would have done anything,

promised her anything, if she would just rub it for me just work me off with her fingers, but then I heard a voice again.

'Well for a slave you know how to lick a woman, I'll give you that. And as a reward I'm going to take the blindfold off now.'

She pulled it away from my eyes and I was puzzled to see she had her knickers, stockings and bra on, she must have slipped them on pretty quick after the service I had given her. And I was thinking why did she do that when a light touch from behind on my shoulder made me jerk my head around and I realised I hadn't been enjoying Eva's sweet pussy at all.

She was almost the opposite of Eva.

Small but almost chunky, muscular even, jet black hair and eyes, she was naked of course and the wetness was still very evident between her legs, her tits were big and her chocolate brown nipples even bigger, and her bush of hair was thick and luxurious. There I was, still tied and helpless, wondering what more could happen.

'I told you I like to watch, Danny. You aren't lucky enough to get to see my pussy and my tits, you'll just have to imagine how juicy my lips are, how good it would be to suck my tits ... But I want to watch you and Diana fuck now. Diana, on your knees, open those sweet legs. You slave, move forward so you can get in behind her. You make sure she enjoys this. She wants to come for us both.'

Eva helped position us as if we were puppets in a cheap show, and as she bent lower she pressed a hand between the other woman's legs and massaged her swollen labia. I was just panting for more. I was praying she would grab my cock and play with me at least a little, but she just manoeuvred us both until I could get inside Diana properly, grinding my pole deeper into her snatch. She had this cute trick of easing her arse onto me and shifting her body constantly so it felt like she was fucking me and not the other way round and boy did it feel good to have her soft wet lips close around

49

my length.

But what made it so much sweeter was the view I had of Eva, sitting back on her sofa, legs splayed wide apart, mouth open in ecstasy, her hand furiously playing between her legs, I could see the moisture pooling even through the fabric of her knickers, I was sure her pussy was freshly shaved which got me even harder.

My thrusts seem to be coinciding with her gasps and movements and I knew I was coming for both of them.

Then it was over. I spurted into Diana's hole, filling her up. I sat back as best I could in my cuffs and saw a look of exhaustion and pleasure on my playmate's features. Eva was breathing deeply too and I just knew we had all come together. I thought even then that maybe I would be allowed to fuck my dream woman. I knew if I dared to speak, dared to articulate my desires for this amazing woman I would never get to make them come true … so I waited and prayed silently.

She gave me that filthy grin again.

'You are allowed to speak, slave boy. Tell me how badly you want to fuck me, how much you would give to get that big thick cock of yours inside my sweet wet pussy. I want to hear you beg for it, grovel and maybe, just maybe you will get lucky.'

And God I did as I was told didn't I? My cuffs handicapped my movements but I was so desperate to please her, to make her relent and let me take her body, I squirmed, whimpered, nothing mattered any more other than me fucking her any way she wanted, her pussy, her lovely arse. 'Please please, please give me a chance, just one chance with you, mistress …'

I saw just how she revelled in me being so totally at her mercy, I had surrendered to her completely and all three of us knew it.

'But what about your little playmate, Danny boy? Don't you think she will be jealous if she has to watch you fucking another woman? I think you should be faithful to her don't you, you little whore?'

Eva paused for a moment. 'Listen to me and remember every word I say …One month from now you will come back here at midnight. You will be wearing a shirt, jeans, no underwear and this …'

She dived behind a chair and produced … for Christ's sake … straight from the medieval age …thick leather padding, stretched around a metal contraption, crudely made but scary enough.

'That's right, slave whore … it's a chastity belt for bad slaves, to teach them obedience to their mistress, let me show you.'

She reached down towards me and I flinched as she roughly grabbed my fast hardening shaft, and pulled, manoeuvred my cock and my aching balls inside the metal and leather gadget. She snapped it shut viciously and then yanked upwards making me cry out as the leather squeezed and constricted my cock. I knew she had deliberately tried to get me to show pain and I hadn't disappointed her, so we both knew I was going to get slapped around. She was savage as her hands cuffed me, but it was over quickly enough.

'You can practice with it all the time until I have you here again. You will wear it all day at work AND at home and don't think I won't check … I can find quiet corners to squeeze your cock and balls. I will know straight away if you are obeying me. I might even turn up at your house one day and when you answer the door, God help you if you aren't wearing it, slave. But if you do as I order, then in a month, you will see what it's like to enjoy me as you want to. If you have played by my rules, you will reap the rewards. Diana may or may not join us – my choice – in fact, slave boy, if you want to learn about pleasure and let me take you to paradise, your days of free will and choice are over. Do you understand? You may speak now.'

'Yes mistress. Thank you mistress. I will wear it as you order me.'

'Good slave. Now, I will release you and you will get dressed and go home and dream of me … and nothing but me. Diana is staying and we will enjoy each other's bodies. Imagine that too, but as you will have the belt on, you will not be able to wank will you? Poor whore. Still, I don't care if that hurts you, it will just make you more ready for when … if … I allow you to fuck me.'

And soon I was on my way home, my head spinning, my cock and balls restrained by this damn contraption. I know it sounds crazy, but I daren't take the risk of her finding me not wearing it. I had stood on the edge of my desires, leapt off the cliff and there would be no going back for me now.

All I wanted was to keep feeling the way this mistress, goddess, whatever the hell she was, had made me feel.

One Night Only? Oh no, no … I had to make sure this was just the beginning of the new Danny. I knew I was born to be her slave and that as long as she let me fulfil that role, I could be happy.

Confessions
by K D Grace

Jilly pushed open the heavy wooden door and peeked inside. The pungent smell of incense and old candle wax brought on that familiar warm tingle just beneath her skin. In the subdued lighting of the vaulted nave, candles flickered on the altar. Her timing was perfect. Her research had paid off. No one prayed in the pews near the front. The few nuns who normally scurried about quietly had gone back to the convent, or wherever nuns went when they were done scurrying about. The only other person in the church would be the priest.

She stepped inside and crossed herself. For a second she stood taking in the atmosphere of the place. It was late now. Her confession would be the last of the night, which was a good thing. She had a lot to confess. She loosened the black lace scarf that lay coiled around her neck and pulled it demurely up over her dark hair so that it settled like a hood about her head shadowing the oval of her face in the soft light.

She wore a full black skirt that swished low against the backs of her calves as she walked up the side aisle, her heels click-clicking on the stone floor. Her black silk blouse brushed softly against her skin. It was modestly buttoned to her throat, yet still it felt decadent in its very caress. The muscles low in her stomach contracted with nervous anticipation. Her pulse hammered against her throat as she drew near the confessional. Oh so much to confess, and she with nowhere else to be, nothing else to do, but seek penance.

Jilly stepped into the confessional and pulled the curtain shut carefully behind her. Then she dropped onto the kneeler and crossed herself. 'Bless me, father, for I have sinned.' She breathed in a layer cake scent of stale perfume and nervous sweat, the delicious remnant of so many people over so many years coming to confess so many sins. 'It's been a week since my last confession.'

'Go on, my child.'

Her pulse quickened at the sound of the priest's voice. She could almost feel the weight of it against the nape of her neck.

She lifted her skirt and sat back on the chair, wriggling her bare bottom against the cool wood. 'I watched my neighbour have sex. She left the lights on, and the french doors were wide open.'

There was silence, so she continued. 'Her lover ripped her camisole off like it was paper. Do you have any idea what ripping silk sounds like, father?' She laid her hand against her breasts and rocked. The chair creaked softly. 'He sucked her nipples, and I sucked my finger tips pretending it was me at her breasts.

'I watched him feel up inside her until she squirmed and begged. Then he ate her like she was ice cream melting on his tongue. Oh father, how I wanted to taste.

'And he nearly split her in two, with his big cock pushing and pumping so hard her breasts juddered and bounced. The room was bright, like a stage, like she wanted me to see. Do you think she wanted me to see, father?'

She heard rustling on the other side of the confessional. Had she made the priest's cock hard? Her pussy tingled at the thought, and she rubbed herself against the chair.

'Perhaps you should close your curtains. Perhaps you should pray.'

'I do, father. I pray all the time.' She pulled an onyx

rosary from her pocket and stroked the smooth beads. Then she wriggled a hand inside her blouse to play with her titties. A little moan escaped her lips.

'Is there more?' the priest breathed.

'I had sex with my roommate's boyfriend. I didn't plan it, father, really I didn't. My roommate was out. At first we just masturbated together, but then I let him put it in me.'

'Dear God.' The priest's breathing was nearly gale force.

'Father, there's more.' She spread her legs wide and rubbed her juices over the hard wood of the chair wondering if the next penitent might get horny sitting in the scent of her arousal.

'Yes?' The priest's voice sounded harsh, raspy.

Jilly wriggled her hand under her skirt and shuddered as her slippery cunt yielded to her fingers. 'Confession makes me come.'

'What?' his voice cracked.

'I can't help it. I always come at confession.' For a second the only sound was heavy breathing. Then the priest spoke.

'Did any of what you've confessed actually happen?'

'Does it matter? As a man thinketh in his heart, so is he. Jesus said if we even look at someone in lust, we've committed adultery in our hearts. He said …'

'I know what Jesus said.'

'Last week, I confessed at St. Mark's. I nearly broke the kneeler. The priest thought I was crying, I was so contrite. I came again during my Hail Marys and Our Fathers at St. Andrew's. I think the priest came too.'

'Our father, who art in heaven,' the priest rasped.

'Hallowed be thy name.' She joined in, rocking in rhythm.

'Thy kingdom come, thy will be done.' The words came faster and faster.

'Giveusthisdayourdailybread!'

Her silk blouse was now wide open and her braless tits

bounced sharply as she rocked. She slipped the rosary over her head and the onyx crucifix smack smacked between her breasts. The scarf with which she had covered her head slipped off and her hair fell loose around her shoulders.

'Forgiveusourtrespassesasweforgivethosewhotresspassag ainstus!' She came hard against the chair, stifling a heavy grunt.

She was wiping her pussy with the scarf when the curtain flew open, and the dishevelled priest stood breathing like a thunder storm, smelling like sex.

He grabbed her scarf and stuffed it in his pocket, then he yanked her up. She was ready. She'd been thrown out of other churches. That, too, made her come. Instead he dragged her to a private chapel just off the nave. There was a bare altar with a painting of Solomon and the queen of Sheba above it. He shoved her to her knees, grabbed her hair, and forced her to look up at him. 'You've made a mockery of the confessional,' he roared.

'Oh please, Father, I just can't help myself. You have to give me penance.'

'Am I supposed to believe you?' He wound his fingers tighter in her hair and pulled her closer.

She wrapped her arms around his legs and sobbed. 'Please. You don't know how hard it is.' His penis twitched against her cheek. She'd never sucked consecrated cock before. Eyes raised, so terribly repentant, she batted her lashes and nuzzled nearer with a soft whimper.

He shifted his hips, almost imperceptibly. Then, rocking slowly, tightly against her face, he prayed, 'Heavenly Father, forgive this child. Forgive her lust, forgive her lewd behaviour.'

The longer he prayed, the harder he pressed her face against his erection.

'Grant her purity in thought, word and deed.'

As he rocked, ever so cautiously, she reached up and unbuttoned his trousers.

He pretended not to notice as she eased down his zipper.

'For all have sinned and fall short of the glory of God.'

His grip tightened in her hair and he caught his breath with a gasp as she tugged his trousers over his hips along with his briefs. His cock practically leapt into her hand.

'Please forgive … please forgive … urgh.'

She took his erection in her mouth, deeper and deeper until he moaned out loud and stopped pretending not to thrust.

She was beginning to fear he had no more imagination than to simply stand there and ejaculate in her mouth, when he shoved away and yanked her to her feet. He pulled the rosary from her neck and with a sharp thwack, slapped it across her tits, just hard enough to sting. 'You're a slut, and you need to repent.' He smacked her again and she moaned as he shoved her blouse off onto the floor. Then he grabbed her tits, squeezing and kneading. The rosary wound around his hand pressed solicitously into the soft swell of her. She arched her back as he suckled and bit her nipples. Pain translated to pleasure in her cunt.

He bound her hands loosely behind her back with her scarf and bent her over the altar. 'Our lives are to be a living sacrifice unto the Lord.' He shoved her skirt up, exposing her arse to Solomon and the queen of Sheba. He smacked each buttock in turn with the rosary, making her pussy clench.

'Forgive me,' she cried. 'Lord, please forgive me.' The beads came down again with a thwack.

'This,' he slapped her pussy with the flat of his hand, 'is consecrated unto the Lord. This,' he smacked her again, 'is the sacred space from which life springs. It wasn't created for lust.'

'I'm so ashamed,' she lied.

He smacked her bottom again with the beads, then he began to pray for her in earnest, grunting with each thwack of the beads.

'Father forgive this woman, purify her heart.'

Thwack!

She cried out and wriggled her stinging arse.

'Purify her mind,'

Thwack!

She practically humped the edge of the altar with every smack. 'Purify her body, so abused by her lust.'

Thwack!

When her orgasm hit, she squealed and bucked and practically kicked the priest in the balls.

He jammed the rosary into his pocket and fumbled and grunted in an effort to press his cock into her pout.

'No so fast, father.' She pushed him away and half fell off the altar, wriggling her hands free of the scarf. 'I think it's about time *you* confessed.' She shoved him against the wall.

'Take off your shirt.' She was already at work on his buttons. 'Take that off too.' She nodded to the collar.

Panting hard, he obeyed.

She slipped into his black shirt, buttoning a single button across the fullness of her breasts. 'Help me with the collar.'

He did as he was told.

When it was securely in place, she scooped up her blouse, then looped the scarf around his neck and tugged.

Holding up his trousers with one hand, while his cock bounced at full attention he followed her into the confessional. 'Kneel.'

He obeyed.

'You've been a very naughty priest.' She slipped off her skirt and stood in nothing but his black shirt and priest's collar and her fuck-me stilettos, then she took his hand and guided it between her legs.

His other hand reached for his cock. She slapped it away. 'I want to hear your confession.'

He took his hand from her pussy and crossed himself. 'Bless me, father, for I have sinned. It's been …'

She slapped his face with a resounding smack, and his penis surged in response. 'I'm not your father. Now do it again.'

He stroked his cheek, which now bore her hand print.

'Do it.'

He crossed himself and started over. 'Bless me ... lady? For I have sinned. It's been twelve hours since my last confession.'

'Go on.'

'I maa ... I masturbated during the confession of a penitent.'

'How?'

'Excuse me?'

'Did you touch yourself through your trousers or did you pull your cock out while this poor girl unburdened her soul to you. Well?'

'I ... I had my penis out.'

'Show me.'

'Please, I was wrong to ...'

'I said show me.'

He blushed mightily, but once his hand was on the meat all shame vanished. He thrust his hips back and forth and stroked like he was rolling dice, his breath coming in hungry gasps.

'What did this sinner confess, father, that so turned you on?'

'That she watched other people do it.' He strained against his hand, his buttock muscles clenching with each thrust. 'That she fornicated, that she ...'

'That she what?'

'That she masturbated at confession.' His voice was as clenched as his buttocks.

She slapped his hand away from his cock again. 'What else?'

He looked up at her dumbly.

'Your confession. What else?'

'I … I ejaculated.'

'Mmm. I can smell,' she said. 'But you're not supposed to do such things.'

'She tricked me.'

'Then you must have kicked her out of the church?'

He shook his head, squirming on the kneeler.

'What then?'

'I let her suck me, then I spanked her.'

'No doubt she deserved it. What else?'

'Nothing else.'

She slapped him again. 'As a man thinketh in his heart, so is he.'

'I wanted to, to have sex with her.'

'You're as sinful as she is.' She grabbed the scarf and yanked him back into the chair. 'I think it's time for your penance. There'll be no Our Fathers, no Hail Marys. I have a better use for your tongue.'

She turned in front of him and bent over until her arse was in his face, then she tugged the scarf, guiding his mouth to her slit. He suckled and nibbled, holding her to him, cupping and spreading her buttocks, licking and stroking until his fingers explored their way, first to her cunt, then, slowly, almost shyly, he slipped his middle finger into her anus.

It felt good, but she wouldn't let him off so easily. She pulled him to his feet and wiped his face on the scarf. Then she kissed him, tasting her pussy on his accommodating tongue. 'Celibacy doesn't look so good right now, does it, Father? But you're not allowed to come until you choose the method.'

'Choose the method?'

'I'm asking you how do you want to come? It's not a difficult question.' Facing him, she guided his penis between her legs, clamped down and began to dry hump him. 'Do you like this? Would you like to shoot your wad this way? Or would you prefer to come in my hand, maybe in your hand? Perhaps my mouth would do it for you?' She pressed down hard so his cock rubbed between her labia each time he humped. 'Or, you can take your chances with the wrath of God and have some real pussy.' She leaned close and licked his earlobe. 'Personally, if there is a god, I think she has bigger concerns than where you spurt your jizz.'

'What about here?' He slipped his middle finger back into her anus so quickly that her breath caught in her throat.

She laughed softly, then she grabbed him by the scarf and forced him to kneel. 'Confess that you want to fuck my asshole, Father, I want to hear your confession.'

'Bless me, Lady, for I have sinned. I want to fu …'

'Say it.'

'I want to fuck your asshole.'

'There, that wasn't so hard now, was it? I grant you absolution.' Then she turned and bent over the chair.

In the tight space, he manoeuvred until her ass was right in his face. He wasn't squeamish. He parted her cheeks, and circled her pucker hole with his tongue, pushing in solicitously. She moaned and squirmed as he inserted a wet finger, then another, moving them back and forth inside to stretch her, stimulating her until he had room for a third.

She groaned at the exquisite pressure and forced her bottom closer to his mouth. Her stretched anus felt like it was on fire. With one hand Jilly finger fucked her pout while bracing herself against the chair with the other.

At last, when her slit thrummed from the stimulation of her backside, he removed his fingers. She heard him spit and felt his warm saliva in her crack. Then with a little gasp, he pressed the head of his cock into her hole. Finally, with a grunt and a shove, he was in, pushing her face hard against the chair that smelled like her cunt.

Then, to her surprise, he began to stuff the rosary beads into her pussy with each thrust until only the crucifix dangled from her vulva. The fullness of her cunt and her asshole, combined with the movement of the beads with

61

each thrust, was beyond maddening. The priest humped harder and faster. His balls slapped against her bottom. With each thrust, he grunted breathlessly, 'Oh God, oh God!'

She joined the chant. 'Oh God, oh God!'

With a thrust that she feared would split her in two, he exploded inside her. At the same instant, he grabbed the crucifix like the pin of a hand grenade and yanked the beads from her pussy. The explosion nearly knocked the confessional over.

When they were dressed again, he kissed the rosary and placed it over her head. 'I can't grant you absolution when I know you're not repentant.'

She chuckled softly. 'I came for the confession, not the absolution.' She wrapped her pussy stained scarf around his neck and drew him into a kiss.

'Will I see you next week?' he breathed when she pulled away.

'Afraid not, padre. There's a church across town I've got my eye on. I hear the priest there believes in heavy penance for sinners like me, and thanks to you, I have so much more to confess.' She sighed and laid her hand against her breasts. 'Heavens. I don't know if I can wait till next week. She turned and walked out of the deserted church.

Doctor's Orders
by Brandon Burnham

I was waiting for Patti in the cool of the lobby bar of the Cross Keys Hotel, Downtown Miami. She'd want to hear all about last week and I reckoned I owed her lunch. I love this girl; she's drop-dead gorgeous, very funny and horny as hell. I guess we're like a really close brother and sister – or would be if it wasn't for the fact that we fuck from time to time, sometimes just because we miss each other, but usually when we're between regular partners, like we were last week when she asked me to come with her to her boss's birthday party.

It had been a perfect day for a barbecue and Patti had eased the drop-head Porsche into a tight space in a driveway packed with money on four wheels. She came round to open the door for me.

'Come on, my hero.'

I managed to scramble out of the car holding bandaged hands out in front. She's a terrible tease and had been enjoying the fact that I couldn't get her back.

'Want a hand?' she taunted.

'Very funny.'

'So next time you save someone from a burning wreck, go get gloves.'

'Thanks for the sympathy,' I replied, pretending to be pissed at her. I shook vigorously so my loose T-shirt could uncrease itself and drop over my shorts. 'I wish I had! I can't do a damn thing on my own.'

'Never mind, I'll help you,' she said, leaning up to give me a kiss while reaching down with one hand to cup my lunch-pack. She turned round without letting go and giggled as she led the way to the door, tugging me behind. 'Let's go eat, I'm starving.'

It was Patrick's birthday and there were about 40 people there to help him celebrate. The massive house was sheer luxury, and so it should be, as the home of a senior partner in one of Miami's biggest law practices. The colonial-style building in Key West Old Town sat in a large carefully tended plot surrounded by mature trees, with a sprawling garden boasting an enclosed barbecue area near the 30 metre pool, where most of the guests were congregated.

Patti had left me to fend for myself and I was doing OK. I could hold a can between my hands, and was enjoying being fork-fed by Patrick's younger sister, Marie, whose stunning body was bursting out of what you could just about call a bikini. At first glance she looked to be about 18, but I could tell she was older than that. Maybe it was the spiky little urchin cut and lack of make-up that combined to knock off the years. She was good company too, making me laugh, and was in the middle of a story about a recent trip to Europe when the beers caught up with me. I needed a pee, and this was something I definitely couldn't manage on my own, so I cast my eyes round for Patti.

'Sorry, am I boring you?' Marie asked, very directly.

'Er no, of course not.' I looked down, indicating my useless hands and then my crotch. 'Excuse me, I have a bit of a problem and need to find Patti.'

'Oh, yeah ... OK,' she said, catching on immediately. 'Maybe she went in. Come on we'll go find her.'

Taking an arm she led me inside. We travelled from room to room with no sign of Patti.

'If she's changing after a swim she'll be up here.'

Taking a left she walked ahead of me up the stairs, bringing my eyes level with the enticing split where her back finished and her ass began. The firm muscles of her buttocks tightened and relaxed deliciously as one foot climbed in front of the other, and it wasn't hard for me to imagine what lay beneath that brief scrap of cloth.

'The guest area is this way.'

With a friendly hand hooked through my arm we made our way along the corridor, and I could feel a breast stroking my upper arm as we walked. Her tits had a life of their own, and nearly burst from the bikini top each time she leaned into a bedroom to call Patti's name. If we didn't find Patti really soon my Bermudas would be showing a lump. An appreciative smile lit up her face as she caught me looking.

'How're you doing?'

'Bursting!'

'OK, well I guess we'd better see what we can do to make you more comfortable.' she ushered me into the last bedroom, pushing me towards an en-suite bathroom. 'Come in here.'

I looked at her helplessly. 'Um, I can't really do anything on my own. I seriously need to find Patti.'

'That's OK, I'm a doctor; you haven't got anything I haven't seen a thousand times before.'

'You're a doctor?'

'Sure.'

'Really?'

'Really, now don't you go telling me I'm too young!' She laughed. 'Everyone does that. I qualified two years ago and now I'm working with kids – which is why you'll be so easy to deal with! Now stop being shy and come over here.'

The prospect of this gorgeous brunette finding my cock and holding it while I took a pee didn't help what I needed to do. I could feel myself getting hard, and with nowhere to go inside my shorts it just made a tent.

I looked down at the pretty face standing beside me, enjoying the cheeky grin which seemed to be challenging me to be brave. I'm not the type to get embarrassed when it comes to having a beautiful woman take a poke around in my shorts, but this different. 'What the hell!' I thought, 'She's doing this because she wants to, not because she has to. I just hope she wants to do something with it afterwards, 'cause she'll need a platoon of Marines to keep me off her.' I smiled back.

'OK, thank you; you're a genuinely kind person. If you just help me with the shorts I can sit and take care of the rest.'

I moved to stand in front of the toilet and she came too. Patti had been helping me out ever since the accident and, though I found it seriously arousing, even she didn't have the same effect as this beautiful stranger. There was no zipper so she had to lean in to pull down the Bermudas. My best friend sprang to attention the minute he was released of course.

'Wow!' exclaimed Marie, unexpectedly faced with my quivering rod, just a few inches from her plump vermilion lips. 'Very flattering, but that isn't going to make it easy. I don't think sitting is going to help much either.'

She stood up next to me and her left arm snaked around my waist while she reached out with her right hand.

'OK, let's try anyway.'

Curling her fingers around the rock hard length of muscle she pulled back gently, slowly revealing the throbbing head.

'Don't want it splashing everywhere, do we?'

Her tone of voice caressed me as much as her knowing touch, and I went from 100 per cent hard to 150 per cent. My cock was like iron, and pointing towards the ceiling. This was definitely not going to be easy.

'I'm not sure I've got a proper grip … just a second.'

Her hand slid forwards until the protecting layer was back in place. Pausing for a second she adjusted her hand before pulling back again – unbelievably slowly. An innocent look sat on her face, but somehow I was sure it was done quite deliberately. This time she drew back as far as the loose covering would naturally allow and then kept going, tightening the thread of skin under the head of my cock until the eye began to bow down.

'That's heading in the right direction,' she murmured encouragingly. 'But there's a long way to go yet. Let me know if I'm hurting you, won't you.'

'Mmm,' I managed to mumble. 'No problem yet, but don't worry I'll shout if I have to.'

Her arm tightened round my back as she began to force my cock downwards. I didn't want to stop – the warm grip was heavenly – but she didn't even manage to get it horizontal before I felt like it was going to snap. It was obvious we were never going to achieve a direct shot into the porcelain bowl waiting below. Reluctantly, I had to surrender.

'Um, unfortunately I don't think this is going to work.'

She let my erection return to its natural position without removing her hand.

'I guess not. What do you think we should do about it? I could leave you alone and you could sit on the pan until everything's calmed down.' She moved her hand up and down, gently milking me as she spoke. 'But that would seem to be a terrible waste.'

Man! This was unbelievable torture! I closed my eyes, letting the weirdly delicious sensations flow through me. The need to pee mixed with horny thoughts sent more blood pumping into my hard-on; making it impossible to do either.

'Just let me think a minute,' I said dreamily. 'I'm sure I'll come up with an answer.'

'Does this help?' she teased.

'Not a bit, but don't stop.'

'What if you use the basin? You won't have to point down so far.'

'Babe, I'm not sure I can make anything happen in this state anyway.'

'Oh dear. Well, as a doctor, I can tell you that's not good

for you; so we'll have to do something.'

'Mmm,' was all I could manage, my eyes remaining closed as her now still hand squeezed me rhythmically.

'OK, I've got an idea.' She bent down and dragged my shorts to my ankles. 'Step out of them.'

I complied and my throbbing weapon danced in front of her face as I moved.

'Think I'd better relax you a bit – but just be sure to behave yourself,' she said sternly, steadying the bobbing pole.

Remaining on the floor she surprised me by slipping her warm mouth over the end. I could feel her tongue racing round in circles before it found the little slit and tried to force a way in, practically making my hair stand on end. 'Oooh, shit that's good.'

Releasing it as suddenly as she'd sucked it in, she stood upright.

'Arms up.'

I did as I was told and she pulled my T-shirt up and over my head, carefully manoeuvring the bandaged hands through the arm holes. As I faced her, stark naked, she stood on tiptoe to plant a brief kiss before turning me towards the shower.

'Can't get this nice new bikini wet' she giggled.' And with a quick movement behind her back she freed her bouncily firm tits, before hooking thumbs into the bottom part and shedding it onto the floor. Stretching a hand into the shower cubicle she twisted the faucet, jumping out quickly to avoid the water, and took up station behind me. I felt erect nipples whisking against my back as both arms stole around my waist, until one hand found the pulsing pole waggling in front of me and the other cupped my balls.

'Hands on head to keep them dry,' she ordered and, as I complied, she nudged me closer to the shower.

'Ok. Let it go.'

'Not very hygienic is it?' I offered weakly.

'Crap! Don't tell me you've never had a pee in the shower – everyone does. The water's running – it's fine so just let it go. Hurry up I've got plans for you.'

Her tone of voice was quite bossy and I got the feeling she was used to giving commands, which was a real turn-on in its own right. Anyway, in the position I was in there was no arguing, so I strained to do as I'd been told. Peeing when you've got a hard-on is not a natural mix, and it took a good forceful squeeze from my internal muscles to get the bladder working. Finally I was able to perform, ejecting the fluids that had started all this, but aware there were now different fluids waiting to go the same way. Normally if I manage to piss when hard, first thing in the morning for instance, then everything goes down quite quickly. Marie was determined that wasn't going to happen, she jiggled my balls, and held my cock firmly until she could feel there was nothing more going through. Finally she gave it a big shake and moved her hand up and down a few times in an expert manner.

'You through?'

'Yes thanks. All done.' I felt about six years old, or would have done if I didn't have a beautiful woman massaging my meat.

Marie reached in to turn off the shower and led me by my pecker to the basin. She held my eyes in the big mirror and turned on the tap.

'Let's just give him a final clean-up then.'

She ran her hand under the water before filling it with soap from the dispenser. Once again her hand circled my length.

'I think we need to work up a bit of a lather.'

She was still watching my face in the mirror as her hand went to work, pumping backwards and forwards, steadily upping the tempo. My eyes left hers and travelled down to where the action was, fascinated to watch the skilful way her wrist rotated as she went up and down, producing a wonderful sensation along every millimetre of flesh. Sure enough she was working up a lather – and so was I. She sensed I might be moving towards the point of no return and released her grip, trailing soapy fingers down to my balls.

'Do you look after these? You should, you know. You need to get very familiar with them to check for changes.' She took it in turns to clasp each sensitive egg, apparently comparing them.

'I'm very happy for you to get familiar with them, Doctor. I think they need a thorough examination.'

She weighed them together. 'They seem very healthy to me, though perhaps they're a little full.'

'Can you recommend treatment?' I asked, prolonging the game as she continued to rub her soapy hands all over them.

'Oh, I think I might have a remedy.'

'Thank God for that,' I exploded.

'But only if you do exactly what the Medic says.'

'Fine by me.'

She rinsed off the soap and reaching for a hand-towel dried me off. She really did have a beautiful body. Firm muscles betrayed a fitness regime, and her full rounded breasts were topped off with provocatively protruding nipples, forcing their way up from a wide surround of matching dark pink. A little vee of close-cropped hair sat at the top of her pussy mound, and from this angle I could even just see the beginning of her cunt lips. She smiled back in the mirror when she spied me sucking in every detail of her body, but, when I reached out for her, pushed away my clumsy cloth-wrapped hands.

'Uh uh! Remember, you just do as you're told,' she said, with a kind of mock sternness.

Reaching for a dispenser of moisturising body cream from the small shelf in front, she squeezed a good handful into her palm and applied it generously all over my dick. The slippery massage was exquisite and I knew I wouldn't last long with much of that treatment. The way she was going I reckoned I would shoot right across the basin very soon, and there would be a trail of jizz sliding down the mirror. But she had different ideas.

'One good turn deserves another.' She smiled seductively, edging us both away from the basin as she moved directly in front of me, facing the mirror. I got forced away further as she bent forward. A slightly more serious look appeared on her face and a greedy tone came into her voice.

'OK, so now you do me in the ass while I play, but do it the way I ask – and don't you dare come before me.'

I love anal sex as much as the next guy, but normally it's something I get round to after dating for a while, and usually instigated by me. To be told to fuck her in the ass before I'd even touched her pussy was a real mind-blaster, I just hoped I could perform without letting both of us down.

With no hands to help, I bent my knees and pushed forwards so the full length of my cock slid between her legs, gliding between the slippery wetness of her outer lips before drawing slowly back, trying to position the head of my cock as close to her asshole as possible. A waste of time! It sprang past the prettily wrinkled target as soon as it could, and Marie had to reach behind to take hold and direct me where she needed it most. Her hand maintained its grip while I pushed forward, pressing the well-lubed helmet against the tight orifice.

'Slowly,' she commanded.

I had a perfect view as my now purple-headed weapon forged gradually onwards, squashing against the resistance in front – aided by the cream, I was definitely making progress in opening up her most secret place – this was the most erotic sight I could ever remember. At last her muscles surrendered, allowing me to ease further in, until finally all opposition was conceded and the entrance burst open to welcome me inside. Incredible! It was so warm – and exquisitely tight. Marie let go of my shaft and moved both hands to her breasts. From her bent over position she looked

71

up into the mirror again to see where the pleasure was taking me.

'Wait!'

I did. She began to massage her breasts and pinch her nipples, savouring the sensation before dropping a hand between her legs. I watched regular waves of movement travel up her arm as she found her clit.

'Now push further in – a tiny bit at a time.'

Following instructions faithfully, I fed my flesh into her, centimetre by centimetre, closing my eyes for a second to focus on the intense sensations as the tight sheath gripped me. She took it all – I was in there to the hilt.

'Wonderful,' she sighed. 'Now move … but gently.'

Resting my useless hands on her hips, and sensing she was as close to coming as me, I didn't want to hurry either. I withdrew almost to the end before gliding back in. But she was hungry and, with fingers working furiously, she began to pant; then a low groan, almost as deep as a man's voice, erupted from way down inside, and I could feel powerful contractions seizing my cock as she started to come.

'Fuck me! Fuck me hard!' she cried. 'Fuck me deep!'

I rammed in and out with a controlled energy as her hand moved franticly, slowing down then speeding up again as she made the orgasm carry on and on. Her eyes closed tightly and suddenly she almost collapsed, letting her head sink down into the basin as she relaxed the assault on her clitoris. I took my cue and slowed right down too, finally stopping to savour the heat, still enjoying the spasms within her as she came down to earth. I just stayed there, saying nothing, letting the moment hang while her senses returned. Eventually she looked up, resting on her elbows; there was a contented smile on her face.

'Good boy. Very good boy.'

She pushed herself upright, leaning back against me but making sure not to dislodge my cock. Her hands came up to her breasts and she pinched both nipples really hard, pressing them out of shape.

'Right big boy … your turn. Give me all you've got, I want to feel you shoot right up to my stomach.'

With a smile of anticipation she bent forward and braced herself for what was to come.

'Go on, give it to me.'

I was only too happy to oblige, starting with long deep strokes, increasing the tempo as I could feel my own orgasm build. Gradually it hit me, creeping up until I was racked with pleasure from the tip of my toes to my scalp, all emanating from the helmet on the end of my cock, and I could feel myself spurt, jetting gallons of hot come deep into her bowels. I began to slow, and could feel her deliberately contracting internal muscles, squeezing out every drop.

Physically and emotionally exhausted I slumped over her back. We were one. After a moment I opened my eyes and jumped with shock when I realised we weren't alone. Framed in the doorway was Patti with a huge grin on her face.

'I guess you won't be needing a ride home then,' she laughed.

'He certainly won't,' panted Marie, laughing too, and apparently totally unperturbed by the intrusion. 'He's not well. He's under Doctor's orders.'

The Strap-On
by Maggie Morton

Percy had noticed the strap-on in her sex drawer instantly. It had shiny silver buckles, pink straps with flecks of gold glitter, and the dildo itself stood at attention, like it was just waiting for someone to slip and fall on it, impale themselves on its very realistic head and just slide right on down until it disappeared inside them, every inch of it enveloped by surprised flesh. Anna had watched his eyes go wide as he saw it, and she'd said, 'Oh, that's only for the bad ones, and the girls.'

Hearing "the bad ones" scared him silly, but hearing "the girls" certainly perked up his ears. He hadn't known Anna was bisexual, he said to her, and she'd said, 'No, I'm *try*-sexual, as in try-anything-once. I've decided no girls for now, and that's why you're here.' Then she'd held up the condom she'd taken from the drawer while he'd been staring, mouth agape, at the strap-on, and he forgot about the strap-on's existence almost instantly.

Only he didn't, not really. Every time he came over to spend the night with her, which happened more and more often, there it was – staring him in the face every time he got out a condom. It was almost like it was taunting him, and then it was almost like it was tempting him, only he didn't really want to admit that to himself. No, *he* was the one who fucked someone's ass, not the other way around. But there it was, always hard, always willing, always lengthy and begging him to, "just try it once. Come on, you just might like it".

Percy most certainly wasn't a try-sexual, or even a bisexual, he was just plain, old-fashioned sexual. And talented, apparently, too, as he could make Anna come and come and come, so talented, apparently, that she had said, 'No one's ever gotten me to do that before,' right after a lovely geyser of fluid flooded the bed beneath her. He'd been more than happy to sleep in the wet spot that night, and he was so very proud of himself.

He and Anna had fucked in every room of the house by the time he moved in, and he found himself continuing to try to up the ante, to keep things exciting for this girl who had implied she had a ton of experience, and furthermore, that she'd had a ton of *experiences*. In their second month living together, he hid his intense study of Japanese rope bondage, then surprised her one night with a coil of thick, black rope, a surprise that she seemed quite pleased with, a completely undisguised look of joy spreading across her face. He'd hogtied her, safety scissors placed on the bedside table like he'd been taught, and she'd made such lovely sounds as he fucked her ass. She'd squirmed around under him, giggling and moaning and then saying, 'Oh, my!' as he slowed down his thrusts, sliding in and out of her with a practiced slowness. She seemed to enjoy being restrained and helpless almost as much as he enjoyed her being restrained and helpless, and he goaded her on, telling her that he could do anything he wanted to her right now, that she was his willing slave, just a bunch of holes to be fucked. She'd really liked that – she'd liked those words so much that he'd told her if she was really good, if she begged, he'd untie one of her arms and let her play with herself while he fucked her ass. She begged for a minute straight, a non-stop trail of words, telling him she'd do anything to be able to get off, and then when she'd promised to even do his laundry for a month straight, he'd cracked up. That was exactly why he loved her.

But still, there it was, all seven or so inches of flesh-coloured goodness, almost like a proffered dessert menu, and even though you're stuffed to the gills, there's a glazed three-tier gateaux calling out your name in the sultriest of tones. Percy had never thought a sex toy could be a seductress (or a seducer, considering what it was), but he started having mouth-watering thoughts of it flit through his head, day and night.

He might be washing up after breakfast or watching a game on TV or even taking a shower, and through his head would flash an image of Anna, wearing his favourite garter belt (the black satin one), encased to the thighs in shiny PVC stockings. She'd be facing away from him, and she'd glance at him over her shoulder, and then suddenly she would turn around, and he'd instantly spot the rubber cock sticking up from her crotch, pointing right towards him. She'd shrug her shoulders, as if to say, 'What am I supposed to do? It's your fantasy; don't you have control over these things?'

And the truth was, of course he did. He also had control over the thoughts of the strap-on that were thrust into his fantasies even while jacking off, thoughts which became more and more common, until it had a starring role in almost every single jack-off fantasy he had. Sometimes, yes, there'd be another woman involved, and she'd be the one it would slide in and out of, slick with the juices of her cunt, while he watched Anna fuck her. Sometimes the girl from the grocery store, or wherever he'd captured her image from, sometimes she'd be wearing the strap-on, and Anna would be the one getting fucked. But most of the time it was just him and Anna, the strap-on sliding in and out of his ass, causing the type of pleasure wet dreams are made of. That was the thought that always made him come the fastest these days, the thought that would make come spurt out of him faster than you can say "dildo".

He didn't tell Anna about these thoughts and so one day when he opened the drawer by their bed to get out a condom he was shocked to see the strap-on was gone. Upon seeing this he let out a very unmanly gasp.

'What? What is it, honey?'

'The … it's … it's gone!' Percy said, the shock and disappointment in his voice so evident that he knew all those fantasies he'd had – all those thoughts of him and her and the strap-on – were written plainly across his face.

'Oh, sweetie! I didn't … I mean, did you want to try that?'

'I …' Percy trailed off. It was already so obvious; did he really need to say it?

The next Friday, Percy came home to work to two packed messenger bags, one his, one Anna's, sitting by the front door. 'I have a surprise for you,' Anna told him, and this was the first thing that had lightened Percy's mood all week. 'We're going on a trip,' she continued, and so Percy, quite excitedly, followed her out to the car, where she blindfolded him as soon as he was settled into his seat. He felt the car pull out of the driveway, and then Anna put on a punk rock mix CD. She, and X, and The Dead Kennedys, among others, kept him company all the way until Anna pulled over and parked. They were probably driving for an hour or less, Percy guessed. Then off came the blindfold, and Percy saw that immediately to their left was a sex toy shop. 'I thought we might need to find a replacement for an item I just threw out,' Anna said, a very sexy grin upon her lips. Percy grinned back.

Inside the store were different sections: one for vibrators; one for the kinkier side of things, crops, rope and the like; and one devoted purely to dildos and harnesses. Once Percy reached that section he was in heaven. Here he would find the strap-on of his fantasies, he was certain of it. 'I want you to pick out whichever one you want,' Anna said, sliding an arm around his back. 'I don't care how much it costs, pick out whatever one you like best. It's an early anniversary gift. For both of us.'

Percy leaned over and kissed her on the cheek, then, slowly, reverently, he approached the display. There were pink harnesses, leather harnesses, vegan-friendly harnesses. And then there were the dildos. There was a long beige realistic dildo. There was a short squat black one, a swirled sparkly red one. But the one that drew his eye the most was one not unlike the one Anna had previously had in her drawer – their drawer, now.

It had matte pale pink straps, lustrous silver buckles, and there was already a dildo attached to it, almost identical to one from a few of his fantasies – it looked to be about six inches long, and was sky-blue, with a subtly realistic head. It. Was. Perfect. Percy could almost feel it sliding inside him, almost sense the amount of pleasure it would bring him once it entered his ass. 'I want *that* one,' he said, pointing to it, and Anna beckoned to one of the sales people, a petite woman with shoulder length, bright pink hair.

'We'd like to buy this one,' Anna said, and the sales woman went into the back of the store, bringing out a mid-sized black box with the dildo and harness proudly displayed behind clear plastic. 'This is our most popular model,' she said as she rang them up, 'I'm sure you'll be more than satisfied.'

Once they left, Anna told Percy that she had rented a small cottage off in the woods north of where they were, and Percy smiled and kissed her hard on the lips. 'You're so thoughtful,' he said, hoping she didn't realise he was saying that only about the gift she'd just got for him. Not that he minded a vacation in a nice (hopefully) cottage for a weekend, but thoughts of the strap-on were taking up almost all of his concentration, and oh my, he was getting hard. They may say that hunger is the best sauce, but "hunger" is just another word for anticipation. He could barely wait till they got there.

The cottage was tucked away from the office where they checked in, surrounded by trees and other lush green vegetation. Anna had chosen a very nice place, Percy thought, and he told her so. He was carrying the overnight bags she'd covertly packed for both of them, but Anna had insisted on carrying the bag from the sex toy store herself, despite Percy's suggestion that he carry it as well. They went into the cottage, which was outfitted with a queen bed covered in white pillows and a quilt, and not much else – a plush, green couch and a few matching chairs sat in an area to the bed's left, but Percy barely even took those in. He was ready. He wanted it. NOW.

'Do you think ...' Percy began, practically hopping from foot to foot in his excitement. 'Could we maybe ...'

'You want me to fuck you with the strap-on, don't you?' Anna said, strutting towards him. 'You want it right now,' she continued, punctuating the word "now" by grabbing his crotch, which would've got Percy's attention even if she hadn't already had every ounce of it. 'You want it shoved into that tight little ass of yours, don't you?'

'Y-yes. Yes, I want it. I've wanted it for ages. I'll beg if you want me to.' And he certainly would too, gladly.

'You won't have to beg,' Anna said, a very salacious grin on her face, and Percy knew she was thinking of something evil to do to him. 'But you will have to give me an orgasm first. Or maybe two, or three, or maybe ...' The look of abject disappointment that appeared on Percy's face made her chuckle. 'Oh, honey, I'm just kidding. Of *course* we'll start with dessert!'

To Percy, it seemed almost as if they were naked in seconds, although he certainly had tunnel vision by now, vision that was directed straight at the strap-on now settled securely on Anna's hips. God, it looked delicious. They pulled back the sheets and blankets together, and then Anna said some very lovely words, at least to Percy's ears. 'What position do you want me to fuck your ass in?'

'How about with me on my back? So I can look at you?' That was the reason he gave her, but really, he wanted to be in the most submissive position imaginable.

He got onto his back, and Anna rummaged around in her bag, taking out some lube and slicking up the dildo with a few very generous squirts from the bottle. Watching her slide her hand up and down the dildo, almost like she was jacking off, well, Percy got so hard it almost hurt. Then she climbed onto the bed, shoved up his legs, and then, finally, he felt the tip of the dildo pressing up against his soon-to-be-de-virginized asshole.

'Now,' Anna said, her voice deep and husky, 'I know you haven't had anything back there before, so I want you to know the cardinal rule of ass-fucking, and that's to relaaax. Breathe deep, and I'm going to start entering you now.'

Percy took a few deep breaths, and lifted his legs a little higher. He was ready, he decided, and so he told Anna to go ahead, to start. And she did, slowly shoving him wide open in a way he'd never been opened before. It was pure heaven. He felt himself, tight around the slicked up dildo, felt every centimetre of it entering him, and then ... it hit his sweet spot, and he found himself moaning like a woman might, the sound high and much more female than male.

'You like that, baby?' Anna asked, reaching up to caress his face.

'Mmm, yes, so much. It feels like ...' and for once Percy knew that words weren't enough to describe what it felt like. There had always been words before, but not now, and so he just shut up, let his voice explain through the sounds he made while she began to fuck him, sliding in and out of the no longer virgin hole, and then more sounds came as she began to fuck him harder. A look came on to her face that showed that their usual roles had suddenly been reversed – she was the one who filled him now, and he no longer held the reins, at least in this moment. And all this time, he had felt the so-familiar sensation of an orgasm building, and he wondered if he was about to find out if a man really could come, just from being fucked up the ass. And then came his

81

answer – an orgasm that was different from all the ones preceding it. One which was maybe even better in certain ways, maybe even better in every single way possible.

When the last shudders and echoes of coming had ceased he opened his eyes, looked up at Anna again.

'Well,' she said, looking incredibly pleased with herself, 'I think we should clean up. Then maybe we could go for a walk. According to the website there's a river down the hill from our cabin.'

She lifted up his arm and kissed him lightly on the hand. 'And then, my darling, I think I might show you what else is in the overnight bags I packed. You know, there are just a few things even more pleasurable than what we just did.'

Percy's eyes widened and then he grinned, because maybe, just maybe, she was right.

Retail Seduction
by Tabitha Rayne

Selena traces the soft fabric over her arm. It feels so luscious and rich she puts it to her cheek, then looks around furtively before winding it around her hands and wrists, lifting it closer to her neck.

'Can I help you?' The assistant appears from nowhere making Selena jump.

'Oh, erm, yes, where are the fitting rooms please?' The assistant looks quizzically at the black velvet scarf which is the only item in Selena's arms.

'It's over there by the lingerie at the back of the shop. You might want to take some other garments in as well, madam?'

Selena nods quickly and grabs the nearest shirt. She makes her way to the changing rooms and tugs at the scarf, which has wound its way tighter around her wrist constricting her hand. It feels good and she takes the tag offered by the changing room assistant.

'Just the two items?' Selena nods again, afraid to speak in case her voice has the tell tale quiver that would alert her and everyone else to her arousal. It always takes her by surprise; it can come from nowhere, but when it does, her need is so great, so overwhelming, that she has to find a place to go, and fast. She scurries to the furthest cubicle and pulls across the heavy curtain. Damn it, she thinks, the only changing rooms in town without a lock …

'My name's Debbie, let me know if you need anything.'

Selena clutches the shirt and scarf to her chest, but is relieved when the assistant wanders off without peeking in. Selena waits, ears pricked, to hear the clack of Debbie's heels retreating back in to the main shop. Paranoia overtakes her and she takes one last peek around the curtain. Nothing. All the other cubicles are empty with the curtains flung back. Satisfied that she is alone, Selena examines herself in the mirror. She looks nervous, frail. It annoys her and she refocuses to the thick black coils snaking their way around her wrist. Her hand is beginning to tingle with the constriction and she carefully unwraps it, feeling the blood rush back in, warm and engorging.

She exhales deeply and fully and looks at herself in the mirror again. That's better. Her posture is now erect but relaxed and her head is tipped back slightly so she is looking down at herself. She breathes in and fills her lungs, her chest, her breasts. She loves watching her own body as it begins its erotic arousal. Her lips are full and red and she watches her tongue glide over them moistening them. She takes the scarf again and pulls it tight between her hands and snaps it taut. As she watches her reflection she imagines she is watching herself through Jim's eyes. She slowly lifts the velvet strap up past her chest, pausing to drag it across her nipples. She smiles as they spring to attention yearning for her to touch them again but she resists and slowly continues the journey to her neck. She lifts her head high and tips it back further tilting it from side to side to examine her slender neck. She rubs the fabric back and forward over her throat, teasing herself. She feels heat between her legs and watches her feet as they move apart, her heels gliding easily over the lino flooring. She has a skirt on; it is longer than she usually wears as she had treated herself wearing suspenders and stockings that morning. She pushes her back into the wall and slides down it slightly to try and ruffle her skirt higher. She manages to get it a couple of inches, but not enough to see the thick black band at the top of her nylons. It frustrates her, but this is part of the game to herself. She can't make it too easy.

She drags her attention back to the scarf and pulls it tighter around her throat, pressing her fists into the cubicle wall. She watches as her cheeks redden and she gasps as excitement floods between her legs. She winds the scarf tighter around her fists and tries, once again, to hitch up her skirt. For every inch it rides up she has to split her legs slightly further apart to keep it there. It's a good pay off. She is practically squatting by the time she catches a glimpse of her suspenders. She opens her knees to reveal her dampening knickers. She wishes she hadn't put them on. Her breathing is becoming a shallow pant and sweat is forming on her forehead and down her back. She squeezes her pussy tight and almost squeals out with the pleasure it gives her to be so hot and turned on by herself.

She reaches the strap and holds both ends in her left hand as her cunt can wait no longer to be touched. Her right hand hungrily yanks up her skirt right up over her bum and hooks it in her waistband. She sits on her crouching heels and spreads her knees as far as she can, all the while pulling and releasing the scarf and licking her lips. The fragrance of her wet pussy drifts up to her face and it makes her desperate. She pulls her panties hard to the side and pauses for a moment to look at the sight before her. A dishevelled horny woman stares back at her with sex in her eyes. She watches as she dives her middle finger into her pussy and brings it out to rub on to her clit. Everything is wet, soaking wet, and she puts two fingers either side of her aching bud and massages, softly at first, then faster and harder. Her breathing quickens and she keeps in rhythm, pulsing the pressure on her throat in time with her finger fucking. Before she has time to catch herself she hears footsteps.

'Are you all right in there?' It is Debbie, the assistant.

'Yes fine, really.'

'It's just you sound like you're having an asthma attack

or something.'

'No, please I'm fine; I'll just be a minute.' The thought of nearly being caught, or actually being caught heightens Selena's want and she releases the strap around her neck. It drops to the floor as she takes her pussy with both hands clenching them in with her thighs trying to apply as much pressure as she can. She holds her breath and crouches stock still and alert, terrified and exhilarated at the thought of Debbie pulling back the curtain. The air is so thick and electric around her she can hear the static deep in her ear canal. She needs to gasp. She needs to gulp in air but she is sure Debbie is still there. She silently grinds her mound into her fists and rubs hard either side of her clit.

It isn't enough.

She looks at the wild look in her own eyes and rises up with her back pressing the wall. Her eye make-up is smeared over her cheeks and her lipstick makes her mouth look raw. She looks like a woman that just needs to fuck. She can't stand it any longer. She releases her lungful of air in a huge wanton sigh and makes a decision. With a dramatic sweep she pulls back the curtain ready to present herself to the waiting assistant. The changing room is empty. For a moment, Selena can't decide if she is relieved or disappointed.

She closes the curtain and turns back to face the mirror. She presses herself against her own reflection and uses all of her bodyweight to press her mound onto her hands. She can see her breath misting up the mirror as she pushes two fingers inside herself. In and out, in and out, she rocks her hips, sliding her cunt on and off her sticky long fingers. Harder and harder she pushes until she can hear her jawbone and pelvis banging against the mirror. Her orgasm surges and she groans until at last her fingers get sucked deeper in with the force of her pulsing come.

'Thank fuck for that.' She breathes on to the glass and wills herself to stand up properly. She stares at herself with wobbling legs and flushed face, hair sticking to her forehead and smiles.

'Are you sure you're OK?' the concerned-looking Debbie asks as Selena wobbles past.

'Yes I'm fine, really.' She smiles as she passes her the shirt. 'This is too small. I'll be taking this though.' She holds up the velvet scarf like a trophy and makes her way to the checkout.

He knew she had been up to something by the way her eyes looked up before she answered any of his questions. She held her hands clasped behind her and bit her lip coquettishly. He half expected if he looked at her feet they would be turned in and twisting about like a child lying badly.

'So where have you been?' He winced at the tone, he knew he sounded accusatory, there was just something about this woman that made him feel like she would dart off at any minute – go wherever her pussy led her, after all, that was how they met. He tried to smooth off the edges of the question, 'I mean, it's horrible outside, I was worried.'

'So you should be worried, I was lost without your big strong presence. Who knows where I could have ended up?' She cocked her head and looked up through her hair at him.

'What do you mean?' He was getting nervous of his own envy and felt his skin redden, out of his control. 'What have you done?'

Selena brought her hand out from behind her back and held it on her delicate outstretched arm. Jim looked at the black scarf dangling from her fingers. She was once again swaying with a devious, no, naughty look on her face. That's it, thought Jim, she wants me to think she's been up to something. He stood up to his full height and breadth and towered over her.

'Just what is that you're holding, young lady?'

'Nothing.' She quickly whisked her hand behind her back

and whimpered a nervous giggle. He reached behind her and grabbed her wrist.

'I said, show me.' He yanked her arm round with force and she gasped. 'What is this?' Jim snatched the scarf with his other hand while he kept a firm grip on her wrist. Her breathing was deep and heady and her eyelids flickered. She was fucking loving this. 'Where did you get this?' he demanded, using a strict voice.

'I took it.' Her eyes widened and he tightened the grip of her wrist.

'What do you mean you "took" it?'

'I stole it from a shop.' He pulled her into him, to let her feel his cock stirring in his jeans. She trembled and bit her lip again.

'So, you obviously need punishing, young lady.' Jim took the scarf from her and examined it. It was crushed and warm from being clutched in her hot sweaty hand. 'Come with me.' He was quite pleased with his authoritarian tone and it had the right effect on Selena who followed him meekly, a far cry from the demanding sexual goddess she'd been the night before. He like this surprising change and decided to take full advantage of this opportunity to dominate.

She stood next to the bed.

'What are you doing over there? Come here.' She took too long and he dragged her by both wrists to the bottom of the bed. 'Since you stole this, you will be punished with it.' He took the velvet strap and roughly bound it around her arms and yanked her forward towards the end of the bed. It was a classic brass frame and she had to lean over as he tied her on to the lowest bar. He liked her pose. Her high heels made her stick her ass out to balance and her back arched making her tits look amazing.

'Do you have anything to say for yourself?' Selena began to turn her face towards him. 'Keep your eyes down, you will not look me.' She returned her head and began to speak.

88

'I ...'

'Shut up!' Jim stopped her, grabbed her hair and leaned into her ear. 'I'm not interested in what you've got to say,' he hissed, then released her head with a nudge.

He looked at her round ass straining through her skirt and smoothed his hand over it. He stood to the side of her and took her hair in his left hand again while rubbing her backside.

'Jim ...' He heard her tiny voice and his reflex was to spank her, he did. She gasped and he knew she wanted it harder.

'I ...' Smack.

'Said ...' Smack.

'Shut ...' Smack.

'The ...' Smack.

'Fuck ...' Smack.

'Up!' He really smacked her hard and the noise left a satisfying slap noise echoing through the room. He worried he might be taking it a bit far as he saw her panting but he caught a glimpse of her lips curl into a grin as she sneaked a look up at him. It made him hard to think she thought she was in control of this. She really was a filthy little madam who wanted fucking every way he could imagine. The future stretched out before him and so did his solid prick. He slid his hand to the hem of her skirt and ran his palm up her thigh.

Stockings and suspenders, no panties. She'd fucking planned it. He curled his fingers into the thick elastic and let it go. She jumped as it snapped back into place. He yanked the skirt up over her reddening ass and examined his work. It had been hard and she had taken it all with delight. Her ass was burning as he rubbed his hand over it and down into her crack. Her pussy was soaking and glistened looking as red and hot as her slapped bottom. He pulled his dick out of his jeans in one swift motion slid it deep into the heat of her wetness. He felt the walls of her pussy twitch around him and knew she was on the brink. He pulled out and watched with pleasure as she followed his retreat with her ass. He wanted her to be on fire.

She was moaning and grinding her thighs together curling her knees back and forth over each other in desperation.

'Please, Jim, for God's sake ...'

'That's enough.' He placed one hand over her mouth while taking himself in the other. 'Is this what you want?' She nodded as he drew his hand up and down the length of his thick prick. Her face strained towards him and she licked her lips. He ran the tip of his head over her lips and her tongue darted over it. He let out a groan as her teeth parted, willing him to let her taste him. He moved forward and she sucked his cock into her mouth hard. She was hungry for him. Her mouth enveloped him and he raked his fingers into her hair and pulled in deeper. Again and again she slid her burning tongue and teeth down his shaft, deeper every time. He could feel her increasing the force, ramming him into her throat and he was ready to explode. He grabbed a fistful of her hair and yanked her head back.

'That's enough!' Jim withdrew and watched her full lips pout and softly smack together. He ran his hands down her arms and impulsively tightened the strapping around her wrists. Her hands were turning white with the pressure and he started to loosen them off.

'No!' Selena's hair was stuck to her flushed cheeks and a wisp had found its way into the corner of her mouth. She motioned to her bindings, 'leave it!' Jim retied the strap and watched as Selena tried to get rid of the hair by first blowing it, then using her tongue. Jim could tell it was irritating her and smiled. He placed his hand back on her ass and slowly traced his palm up over the fabric of her skirt straining over her buttocks.

At the waist band, he pulled out her blouse and ran his hands round her middle and up to her breasts. She shivered and he eased the top of her bra down releasing her turgid nipples. They gently bounced and he squeezed the swollen mounds together, massaging the hard nipples between his finger and thumb. She was grinding her hips and ass again into thin air and Jim could smell her frustration. He took his hands away and gently tugged the hair from her lip and cheek.

His cock was aching, it was getting too much for him to resist and he took his position behind Selena once again. Her hips thrust backwards into him and he spread her buttocks apart with both hands. He couldn't wait any longer and thrust right into her, jamming his pelvis into her ass cheeks. They both groaned, pussy and cock twitching and bucking. He pulled out slowly and dived back in. It was hot and soft and luscious and his dick had never felt so slick. As he kept on sliding himself in and out of her engorged pussy he reached around to her ripe clit and she gasped as he rubbed it with his soaking fingers.

They fucked harder and harder until the surge of come was too much and Jim slammed himself into the very centre of Selena. She let out a shriek as he shot his love deep into her twitching pussy and they slid to the floor together panting.

Later, as Selena gently folds the scarf and puts it away, she takes the receipt from her purse and quietly throws it in the bin with a small smile.

Have Your Cake and Eat It
by Jeremy Smith

The kids had gone, leaving a mess of balloons and plates; all that was left to do was clean up the village hall before the W.I. turned up. I enjoyed catering but it was always a bit annoying to see so much food go to waste, maybe jelly and custard were out of fashion, replaced by healthy carrots and celery.

Leigh, my boyfriend, scurried by with another bag of rubbish, he was helping me tidy up so we could get back quicker, he didn't need to say why, but I knew. The big giveaway was the bulge in his tight jeans that had been getting bigger all afternoon. Not that I minded, the sight of it turned me on, it gave me a warm feeling just below my stomach, the one you get when you know that someone is lusting after you. He'd been away working for a week so I knew he was going to be really desperate for it, nearly as much as I was. In fact, I couldn't wait to feel him slide his hard shaft in me and I had taken any excuse I could to accidentally rub against it when I passed him just to see if I could make it bigger. He knew I was teasing him and loved every second of it.

In some ways it was good when he was away because it gave him time to fantasise about me and he'd get so worked up he'd come back with the kinkiest of suggestions. I'd been tied up, spanked, we had set up the camcorder and watched ourselves have live sex. One time we even went online so all the world could watch, and by the amount of comments we

93

got I think that most of the world did. A threesome was one I had yet to build up the courage to do, I had thought about it enough and with both sexes. Of course Leigh wanted two women and although it would be exciting to explore another woman's body, there was something about having two cocks that sort of fascinated me.

The sex on the beach had been great, and the time we joined the mile-high club in that airplane toilet had been quite acrobatic.

Leigh certainly liked his kinks.

One of my favourites was changing room sex, I would take some clothes into a shop cubicle and he would follow and pull the curtain across. To know there was only that thin material between us and the outside world was such a turn-on and of course you couldn't make a sound in case you were heard. I would bend over for him and he would just lift my skirt up and pull down my knickers and he'd be inside me like a chased rabbit down a hole. Hard, fast and fantastic and we would be back outside before his come had finished trickling out of me. I smiled and wondered what little depraved fantasy he had lined up for me this time.

I hurriedly started to gather up the bowls of food, a bit too quick and spilt some strawberry drink over my blouse – that stain wouldn't come out unless it was soaked – so I started to unbutton my top when Leigh came in.

'You starting without me, Julie?' He smiled hopefully.

'No. I spilt some drink on it,' I took my blouse off revealing my white lace bra, of course his eyes looked straight at my breasts as they jiggled above the cups.

'There's some juice on your neck.' Leigh bent in closer, lowered his face and gently sucked up the drips. His breath was warm and his tongue moist, a shiver went down my back and my nipples erupted against the tight lace material. God it felt so good, especially after a week's separation.

His hand moved to my bra and he gave me a testing squeeze, I pushed my nipple against his palm.

'You like it when I nibble your neck then?'

'Mmmm,' was all I could answer.

He dangled his fingers in the juice pitcher and sprinkled some more onto me. Again his mouth followed the drips, this time along my shoulder. He pushed his hips against my thigh and rolled the hardness of his cock against it.

'So is it just juice you like dripped on you?'

'As long as you lick it off I don't care.'

'In that case!' He reached for a jug of custard.

Before I knew what had happened he had put a dollop of custard into my cleavage and began to lick it out, burying his face between my tits as he squeezed them together, snaring his nose. To feel his tongue flick against my body was sending shivers all over me. I wondered how much custard he had. I undid my skirt and let it fall to the floor. I needed him to lick more than my cleavage.

It took a moment for him to realise that I was standing before him in just my bra and panties, but when he caught site of the tight material stretching over the mound between my legs his smile widened.

'What's going on here?' he said.

'You have the custard, you tell me.' I smiled back at him wickedly.

He ran a finger down my stomach and onto my panties, I held my breath as he traced it along my furrow making me squirm, making me want him even more.

'You're so wet,' he said. 'Anybody would think you've been having dirty thoughts.'

'The same ones you're having.' I pushed my breasts out towards him. 'Get me sticky,' I demanded.

He didn't need telling twice. He raised the custard jug, pulled open one of my bra cups and filled it with the creamy yellow liquid then let it snap back onto me. I gave a sharp intake of breath, the custard was cold as it squidged out over my tit. He took it in his hand and gave it a rub, custard oozed out through the lace as his hand drew over it. He opened up my other cup and filled that one, then squashed that on to me, cold and wet he rubbed it.

'How does that feel?' he asked, still massaging.

'It feels … nice … dirty. I like it.'

'Good, because I haven't finished yet,' he said as his cock throbbed eagerly at me through his jeans. 'Take your bra off.'

I undid the clasp at the back and even with the straps off my bra was stuck to me. I slowly peeled it down, the custard trying to suck it back to my skin. He prised it off over my nipples and threw it onto one of the tables. My breasts bounced free before him impatiently heaving for more attention, although already coated he poured more on, smearing it over with his hand, drips flicking from my hard bullets, it felt a bit like when you spread cold after-sun on but more so, sweeter. My tits slipped in and out of his hand as if trying to escape and when he caught them, flesh and custard moulded between his fingers. Drips fell on to my stomach and he bobbed down to angel kiss them off. He dripped more on me and it felt divine, each spot a cold teasing sensation sending my muscles into spasm.

He took a teaspoon and filled it, then he flicked it at me splashing it over my stomach, the coolness tensing my muscles. I imagined it was his spunk spraying on me.

'Undo my trousers,' he commanded. 'Get my cock out.'

I reached out, yanked at his zip, he wiggled as I pulled down and he kicked his jeans to one side of the hall. His dark boxers were already stained with a silvered trail of pre-come, his cock jutted forward trying to push through the material. I knew my own knickers were just as damp.

'You gonna fuck me now?' I asked, still thinking about his spunk.

'Oh no. Playtime isn't over.' He grinned as he stared at my tits. 'On your knees.'

I obediently knelt down.

'Squash your tits together.'

I put a hand either side of them and pushed, my cleavage became deep enough to get lost in. Leigh reached for the custard again and poured it down the dark valley, then he manoeuvred himself in front of me, and slid his cock straight between my sticky mounds. His coated yellow knob appeared between them, slowly he pumped away at my chest and I tightened my flesh around him. Each time his cockhead appeared I dabbed it with my tongue licking it clean of its now sugary pre-come.

'God that feels good,' he sighed, sliding his whole length in and out. 'It's almost as slippery as your pussy.'

He had such a look of contentment on his face that I wondered if he was going to come there and then and splash his load over my neck and chin. I opened my mouth, half expecting to catch his salty jism but instead he slipped out. His hand snaked between my legs and touched my swollen pussy, testing the waters.

'Your knickers are soaking,' he said. 'And you're so hot.'

'I really need a fuck,' I half pleaded.

'Better cool you down a bit first.' He took a plate of jelly from the table and with one hand he pulled open my waist band, with the other he grabbed a fist full of jelly, his hand shot into my knickers and cupping between my legs he pushed it onto me making me squeal. If I'd thought the custard was cold this was something else. He slowly circled his palm against me, smearing the sticky coldness over and between my lips. Goose pimples erupted over my body and as he slipped a sneaky finger inside me, I squealed again.

He pulled his finger out and sucked it.

'Mmm, you taste of strawberries,' he said and then emptied the rest of the plate into my knickers. It was so cold against my burning heat I half expected to see steam as the melting lumps were held tight against me by my damp lace.

'Walk about,' he said.

I stood up, my knickers bulging with jelly, a small run of it trickled, ice-cold, down my thigh. I moved some more and let it squelch around between my legs. I bent over to show him my arse and it squelched up into my hole, cold and tingly.

'You're enjoying that, aren't you?' he murmured.

'More than you know.' I shivered and rubbed my hand between my legs pushing it tight to my clit.

I saw another jelly on the table, complete out of the mould. I took it on the dish over to Leigh and I pushed two fingers deep into it making a scarlet slit in its wobbly surface.

'Your turn,' I said. He looked at me puzzled for a moment. 'Fuck this.' I grinned at him.

For a moment he just stood there, then he took his cock in his hand and with the jelly held at thigh level he slowly guided it into the hole I'd made. I could see it slide in through transparent sides, his foreskin pulling on and off as he fucked it.

'Oh. That's freezing!' His eyes widened.

He pushed himself in and out of the cold pussy I'd made. Each time it slurped and sucked, wobbling the whole plate. His thrusts make my tits wobble in time with it. His balls slapped against the smooth surface, contracting against the cold shock but if anything his cock got bigger. I can't explain why, but watching him fuck the jelly really aroused me. Given the chance I think he would have kept going, but under his onslaught it started to disintegrate.

We were both into this new kink now and looked around for some other depraved way to use the food.

'Chocolate gateaux,' he said. 'I'm going to eat it.'

'How is that kinky?'

'Well, Julie, I'm going to eat it off your pussy.'

He walked to another table, his pendulous cock swinging in front of him, when he returned he put the cake on the floor. I looked down at it covered in cream with cherries on top.

'Take your knickers off, squat down and sit on it,' he

said.

My undies now felt like they were glued to me, stuck firm by the jelly but with a gentle tug and a wiggle they slid down my legs and puddled at my feet. I kicked them away and they flew through the air, slapped against a window and stuck to it.

I stood astride the cake and lined myself up. Slowly I lowered myself down. When I hit, it was like sitting on cool mud. I sank in and felt the cream work its way up my bum cleavage, as it pressed at my holes my arse puckered against the chill. I started to sway my hips, grinding myself down into it, squashing it into a chocolaty mess between my thighs. It felt so good, so dirty. I thought about climaxing as he watched me get off on this cake, watching my cunt messier than I thought possible. This sex really was dirty.

I put my hands behind me on the floor and raised my stomach, with my legs wide apart I presented him with the chocolate delight.

'Eat me out then,' I told him.

He got on all fours and his face fell onto my sex. Greedily he licked and ate, letting his tongue clean out every hole and fold of skin, he buried himself into me flicking at my clit sending shivers down my neck and along my back. He kept licking even when the cake had gone, pushing his tongue deep inside me. The cake must have been good but I knew he liked my juices better and right now it was dripping from me.

I looked down my food-streaked body, the custard on my tits, the jelly and cake that clung to my pubes, and then I looked at his face still between my legs as he ate away and I just had to have more of this messy sex. I wanted to have the stickiest most slippery fuck possible. I let him lick me for a while longer, feeling the energy build up in my stomach, my muscles began to tighten as my orgasm started to grow, but I was just teasing myself, I wasn't going to let myself come yet, I wanted this one to be a screamer. I moved away from him and then pushed him down.

'Lie on your back,' I said.

He lay flat, all apart from his manhood that flexed in the air. I grabbed a handful of custard and slapped it onto his cock, watching it slide down his thick veined shaft. Slowly I started to wank him, working the custard all over, rubbing it over his exposed knob, a dribble of pre-come mixed in. I grabbed another dollop and splashed it onto his balls, and rubbed them as I wanked. He arched his back and pushed himself into my fist, groaning. I knew he wanted me to go faster but I kept it slow, I was going to bring him to the boil gently. This had to get far messier before I would let him climax. I eased his foreskin up and down, stretching it tight then back over his knob. his groans increased each time. Then I released his balls and started to give him a double hander, twisting each hand in opposite directions as they went up and down. I could almost see his balls grow heavy as he readied his load.

'Not yet, Leigh,' I whispered.

I reached out for the custard jug and tipped most of it over his cock and stomach. Then I straddled him and lowered myself down, he watched as the pussy he had just freshly cleaned descended onto him, and his cock lay flat underneath me.

'What're you doing now?' he asked.

'I'm going to rub my pussy all over you.' Slowly I eased my way forward, feeling his cock slide between my pouting lips. A wave of custard pushed along with me, over his stomach and up to his chest, my pussy leaving a trail behind it. I swayed my hips backwards and forwards, dragging my clit along him, teasing it against the rough hairs of his chest. I slipped and slid all over, getting messier and messier. I moved back down to his cock, letting his knob just ease its way to my hot entrance and then I pulled away. I lowered myself onto him further down his shaft, and slowly masturbated myself against his throbbing hardness as he flexed and bucked against me. I was so near to coming, but I didn't want this feeling to end.

I grabbed for the rest of the jelly on the plate and dropped it on his chest. I lowered my chest down and rubbed my tits into it, my achingly stiff nips massaging against his. I took hold of one breast and squashed it forward for him, red jelly stuck to it ready for him to lick away. I offered it to his mouth and he sucked me inside, stretching my nipple out. He clamped his teeth around it, sending a sharp exquisite spark all the way through me. Then, still held between his teeth, he flicked the end of it with his tongue. He released me and looked at my other tit. I held it tight in my hand and pushed it into his face, jelly smeared across his cheek and chin before he opened his mouth and clamped down on me. God that felt good.

'Suck it,' I sighed. I was pulled in deeper, feeling the blood rush to the skin. He nipped at me.

'Bite it.' His teeth chewed painfully on me, almost more than I could bear. 'Harder.' I squealed with delight and rubbed my cunt against him, squashing my puffy mound hard onto his cock. I pushed more tit into his mouth, and with my free hand I reached behind me and fondled his custard-sticky balls.

'I'm going to fuck you so hard,' he said.

'You'd better.'

'I'm going to stretch that pretty little cunt of yours wide open.'

'Yes, yes.' I rubbed against him harder, feeling his cockhead edge towards my opening. I sat up on him and his hands reached for my breasts, pulling at them, tweaking my already red nipples, stretching them out and pinching them.

'Say you want me to fuck you, Julie.'

'Fuck me, fuck me hard,' I panted.

'On your knees and bend over. Let's do this properly.'

Hurriedly I dismounted him, got on all fours and with my head on the floor I stuck my arse high in the air, my puffy

101

lips pushed out from between my thighs already open and inviting as I moved my knees further apart.

'You look so sexy,' he whispered. 'Just one more thing to finish the picture.'

The next moment, instead of feeling his cock push into me, I felt more custard being poured at the top of my arse cleavage, it slowly flowed south over my arse hole and down to my pussy, for a moment it seemed to linger there then I could see it drip off and puddle on the floor. I saw Leigh's face lower towards me, and starting at my pussy hole he licked all the way back up my cleft, and over my arse until he had licked and cleaned the whole channel. With his tongue gliding over both my holes I felt like I was going to explode. I pushed myself back onto him in the hope his tongue would go deeper but then he moved and I held my breath for what I had been waiting for.

He eased my legs wider apart and then I felt his cock begin to nudge at me, finding my secret path to my velvety depths. Once at the entrance he leant forward, and pushed his way inside, his thick swollen member widening my passage to accommodate its girth. I moaned loudly as I felt his balls began to slap against my clit as he pounded his way in, faster he went. His hands gripped at my hips, slipping on custard. Deeper he went, I started to feel light headed, my heart pounding as my tits swayed to and fro. I ground myself against him, meeting every thrust. My moans became more like a whimper as I waited. I clenched my fists as the sparks danced in my stomach and then it happened, like an explosion in my mind I came. I yelled out and still he thrust into me, pumping harder and harder, in and out of my sloppy hole, I yelled some more until gradually the feeling began to subside, but I kept the momentum going for him. Leigh began to groan as well, I looked at him over my shoulder, he was biting down on his lip, his eyes closed in concentration. Deep inside me I could feel his cock begin to jerk and buck against my tight muscles. Then, if possible, it began to get stiffer. I reached a hand back between my legs and let his balls rub against my palm and he drove forward, they were hot and heavy, hanging low as they swung.

'That's it, fuck me, stretch me,' I urged him on.

He opened his eyes and looked at me. He mouth fell open as he was about to come and then he pulled out of me, took his juice coated cock in his hand and aimed at my arse. A long stream of come shot out of him, splashing onto my cheeks, then another, this time between them, running down my crack and onto my pussy, then one more. Breathing heavily, he rubbed his cock and one last gush covered me. For a second he looked proudly at the mess he had made and then with a smile he rubbed his come all over my cheeks.

'Perfect,' he said.

'The best,' I replied with a giggle.

From the back of the hall came the voice of a little old lady. 'Don't stop on our account,' it said.

Shocked I looked over as an audience of several elderly women stared at us.

'Would you like some jam on that?' One of them held up a jar in her hand and smiled at us.

104

Spankilicious
by Alcamia Payne

Recently Colette had been experiencing a sense of desperation. On awakening from her spankilicious fantasies she seemed confused and as if her life had lost its direction.

One particular morning she work up from a terrible dream and when she looked in the mirror she saw her normally lustrous eyes seemed duller and her skin had assumed a grey pallor. For some reason the fire of her sexuality had been dampened and as she sat on the side of the bed she felt as if there was nothing kinky enough to relight her fuse.

The trouble is, Colette ruminated. I've reached the point of sexual satiation and I'm immune to arousal.

Colette's kinky explorations with spank had started with a single slap, and that slap had flicked the ignition switch within her sex which was enough to send her on a heady spiral of female ejaculatory delight. She derived intense pleasure from having her tight little butt cheeks spanked and her hair pulled until her eyes watered. But, before long a simple spank failed to satisfy her, and Colette sought out masters known for their psychological control, and their skill with paddles and whips, as she demanded ever more violent spankilicious sessions.

Colette thoughtfully fingered her bottom lip. Oh yes, she needed to be slapped until all her metaphorical sexual valves were turned on, and she was teetering on the verge of orgasm. Lately, however, she required more of a perverse, spankilicious thrill than even that. She yearned for an injection of divine kink.

'It's like a surfeit of chocolate or too many drugs,' she explained to Maxine, who acted as her informer within the world of fetish kink. 'Too much of it simply deadens you and then you fail to reach the requisite high. The truth is, darling, simple spanking doesn't do it for me any more. I need something else.' Colette was pacing her lounge like a caged lioness. 'I need some edge from a true kink maestro. I want a man who doesn't just play at domination like he plays a round of golf. I want a man who feeds his desire like an obsession. Now, Maxine, there has to be a spankilicious master out there, who can give me a fix. Find him. Dig deeper.'

Soon Maxine came to Colette with an interesting piece of information.

'I've found him,' she said triumphantly. 'They call him Jouet and he uses a hair whip.'

Colette experienced a frisson of sexual interest and the return of the ripening wetness between her legs.

'Women go crazy for him, and the tales about his whipping skills are legendary.' Maxine elaborated. 'They want to fondle the hair whip and hold it on their fannies. He's a true pervert, a fetishist of the first order.

'So how do I catch his eye?'

'Well that's the tricky part. Forget all those pervy guys you used to hang around with. They're just amateurs. Jouet takes sadomasochistic multi-orgasmic subbies only. I'm told his goal is to make women scream with euphoria and he really gets off on it.'

'Ooh la la!' Colette exclaimed, smiling to herself as her nipples firmed into hard points, and she curled her long, extravagant hair around her fingers. 'He sounds just the one for me.'

'Remember when we were in the club the other night and you pointed to that girl called Maybelline with the short hair, which you said looked as if she'd taken an industrial shaver to it?' Maxine raised an eyebrow. 'And then you singled out Celeste, that black girl with her bleached bob. Well, they have one important thing in common. They were once Jouet's girls. You'd have to be certain all that whipping excitement warranted the loss of your beautiful hair though, because he has a serious kink about long-haired women and he scalps his subbies and plaits their hair into the hair whip before using it on the next victim. He believes the whip carries an erotic charge and with each additional scalp, its sexual potency gets stronger. Moreover, the harder he uses it, the faster the energies flow and each new girl gets an even more intense orgasm. Now, did you ever hear of anything so far-out?'

'Crap,' Colette said, shrugging her elegant shoulders.

Secretly though, Colette trembled at the thought of Jouet and his hair whip, and for the first time in ages, her sexual aridity was sprinkled with the juices of arousal.

The following day Colette went to the Blue Palm Club where she followed Celeste into the women's room. 'Celeste.' She smiled. 'You were Jouet's girl weren't you?'

Celeste was peering in the mirror as she applied her lipstick. 'Yes. Why?'

'So,' Colette said. 'How would I go about being chosen?'

Celeste shrugged. 'It's hard to be chosen by Jouet and very difficult to please him. When he eventually decided to consider me, I had to stand in front of him naked and let my hair down. For him to take you, your hair has to be in excellent condition, natural and very long, and strong enough to take all the vigorous punishment of his tugging and pulling. Furthermore, he always measures it with a ruler to make sure it passes the statutory 26 inches, from crown to tip. Then he probes every strand like a scientist in a laboratory testing it for quality and strength. Jouet enjoys being turned into a beast through the alchemy of the hair and his prospective slaves know instantly if they're on his short list because his cock rises to the occasion. Once, a girl was so desperate to be chosen, she resorted to trickery. She purchased hair extensions and Jouet really lost it. He's quite …' Celeste sighed. 'Tempestuous. But delightfully so.'

'How fascinating.' Colette urged. 'And I've heard rumours about orgasm. Did he ever beat you to the point of orgasm?'

'Oh! Of course.'

Colette admired her body in her cheval mirror. She was exceedingly attractive and while not thin, she had curvaceous well-proportioned limbs and pale soft skin. However, Colette's most outstanding attribute was her gorgeous long hair, which she only ever washed in fine herbal shampoos and allowed to dry naturally, so the ends never became dry.

This particular evening, she brushed it until it gleamed and since it was very hot, she clipped it back in combs and slipping into a skirt which showed off her shapely legs, she set out once again for the Blue Palm.

Jouet was hard to miss. He had the appearance of a wannabe rock star with his sinuous body encased in shiny black leather, his sexy half-lidded eyes and goatee beard woven into a plait.

He even looks like a whip, Colette mused, as her heart beat wildly and she wondered if his cock was as flexible as his whip.

Moving onto the dance floor, Colette unfastened her hair and shaking it loose around her shoulders she began undulating her hips to a sexy salsa.

Soon Jouet moved up behind her and as they completed a slow sensual circuit of the dance floor Colette felt Jouet caress her hair.

'I like you,' Jouet said, pressing his mouth in her thick waves. 'You have the hair of an angel.'

***

In due course Jouet called Collette and asked to see her.

She chose a simple dress, which hugged her body and she wore nothing underneath, so should she become aroused, her nipples would show and her juices would mark her clothes and thus demonstrate to Jouet the possibility of her exceedingly wet and copious orgasms.

When he answered the door he was coolly implacable, his gaze lingering on her shimmering mane of hair.

Well, he certainly knows how to do things in style, Colette thought, as she strolled into the sumptuously appointed modern apartment, before sitting down on a plush sofa. Then Colette unfastened her hair clip and again shook out her hair so it fell in a rich cascade down her back.

'Men love my hair. I ought to get it cut because it's so difficult to manage, but I can't bring myself to do it.' She sighed. 'My previous lover bought me an antique dressing table set. He saw me as a Pre-Raphaelite princess and he worshipped my hair.'

'I can understand why,' Jouet remarked as he tugged on a strand of her hair and powerful electrical frissons pulsed up and down Colette's spine.

'And before you ask, Jouet.' She turned her glittering and perspicacious gaze on him. 'It's all mine, every last strand. I've always had long hair since I was a child. Mummy didn't believe in little girls having their hair cut and she used to delight in plaiting it and putting it in stupid ribbons and showing me off to her friends. Later on, I discovered if my mother tweaked a strand or pulled the elastic band too tightly, I experienced a twinge of orgasmic rapture. Even now, I can remember leaning over the kitchen sink and mother pulling the comb through it. Delightful, simply delightful. And you'll notice it's in fabulous condition, I never blow-dry it and I don't believe in ghastly synthetic colorants.'

'And there are no extensions at all? You understand the penalty for that little trick don't you?' Jouet asked, sotto voce, as he thoughtfully stoked his beard.

'I couldn't afford those,' Colette lied, although the fact was Colette had an excellent job and she could well afford it.

'You've got great potential, my darling.' Jouet grinned maliciously. 'Most women try and lie to me. You do realise long hair's a little fetish of mine and I get super-horny over it, don't you?'

'Indeed. I've heard all about you,' Colette replied, raising an exquisitely manicured eyebrow. 'You used to be a circus performer in a French Circus and they say you come from gypsy stock and that you have a volatile temperament.'

'Yes, my sweet. My family were masters of the whip and there isn't a trick I can't do with it. Why if you want a demonstration, I could flick a coin off the floor and into your hand.' Jouet smiled wickedly, his eyes glittering with innuendo.

Colette felt a smouldering sense of satisfaction as she cast a sidelong glance at Jouet. She loved passionate personalities and there was something incredibly sexy about Jouet's lean rock star body and angular features. Add a dangerous pinch of kink and a squeeze of carnal spank with the infamous hair whip, and you ended up with a powerful recipe. Colette shivered and her nipples stiffened against the flimsy fabric of her dress.

As Jouet circled her like a bird of prey, Colette thought they could have the most amazing relationship. Just the touch of his fingers started her juices running and her cunt pulsing. Twisting her hair tightly around his finger, Jouet laughed cruelly as he brutally twisted and pulled on her hair.

'I wonder if you're willing to make the ultimate sacrifice.' He gave her hair another ferocious tug. 'You must ultimately give all of this up for me. There's no use weeping and wailing when I give the command.'

'Oh!' Colette said wryly. 'I'm selling my soul, or rather my hair, to the devil, am I?'

'Yes, darling, you could say that. I demand inviolable rights over your trichological bounty. Women fight to have their hair included as a trophy in the hair whip.'

'I have no issues with that.' Bowing her head Colette felt such a tremor of clitoral excitement she had to clamp her legs fiercely together as beads of sex juice began to dribble down her leg.

'Now …' Jouet tweaked her hair so harshly a few strands came away in his fingers and he placed them in a small plastic packet. 'I require a small sample for analysis.'

Colette was quivering from the violent stab of pain and her eyes were watering, but she had such sadomasochistic tastes, the pain only aroused her.

'You do realise my whipping can be quite vicious at times?'

Colette shot Jouet a suggestive glance from beneath her sumptuous lashes. 'I can take whatever you hand out, and the harder the better. Actually, I've got a huge pain threshold. The harder the spank, the more I come, and I have plenty of this to go around.' She stroked her hair invitingly.

Jouet lent closer, brushing her cheek with his lips. 'God, it really is the most fantastic hair I've seen in ages. It makes me so horny I could start whipping you right now.' And, as if to confirm his intentions, Jouet wrapped his fingers around a wavy lock and jerked it so savagely a sexual spark detonated – rapidly travelling the highway of Colette's neural synapses to cause an orgasmic pulse deep in her sex. Colette gave an, 'ah' of appreciation.

'Maybe I ought to whet your appetite.' He laughed. How would you like to see my whip, angel?

'What makes you think I want to see your fucking whip?' Colette retorted, challengingly.

'My, you've got a mouth on you. I like a bitch who answers back and talks filth. I may let you lick it, and if you're a really good girl, I may shove it up your cunt and you can see how a fucking whip, or should I say whip fucking ... really feels. What do you think about that?'

'What makes you reckon I want it up my cunt?'

Jouet smirked. 'You invite a spanking, and a hard one. Now, for your insubordination I won't let you see the whip just yet. I'll simply let you salivate over the thought of its delights.'

Jouet often beat Colette with a paddle or his hand. However, he never struck her with the whip and in fact Colette never even got to see the source of her fantasies. Over the weeks she'd become much more submissive and she'd learnt that Jouet enjoyed his girls begging for a flogging, so in her desire to see the whip and have it thrash her cunt, she was now ready to agree to practically anything.

One day she visited Jouet and he said, 'Colette, my precious. I think that finally I've broken the horse. Tonight you'll do exactly as I say, won't you? Peel off that very pretty dress and let down your hair.'

Reaching for her zipper, Colette allowed the dress to fall from her shoulders, revealing her naked body and her buttocks which were still pink from her last beating. Next, she loosened her abundant hair, letting it fall forward in a scarlet waterfall.

'Very good. Lean across the chair, whore.'

Jouet slapped her with the palm of his hands until her buttocks were red raw, but this failed to satisfy Colette and she cried out, 'Please, Jouet I beg you. Bring out the whip. Please! I'll do anything, anything at all. I think I've waited long enough, don't you?'

'So you'll let me beat your pretty little breasts with the hair whip and even your fiery thatched cunt.'

'Yes, Jouet. Anything, anything.'

With a salacious smirk, Jouet fetched the whip and held it up for her to see. It had a polished wooden handle, carved in the shape of a penis. The most amazing thing though, was the lash which was fashioned out of plaited hair of every conceivable shade.

'You may touch it.' Jouet said, placing it in her hands. 'I want you to feel it and then you can imagine how the hair whip will feel on that sensitive skin of yours.'

Colette trembled with lust and her womb went into a series of clutching spasms as she held the whip to her lips.'

Jouet grinned. 'You're extremely privileged, Colette. See how long the whip is? Any longer and I won't be able to manage the lash.' Jouet caressed the whip. 'I tried to include every shade of hair in it, but your perverse outrageous shade will be the finishing touch for the tip. Kiss and make love to my whip, honey.'

Colette did so and the taste of the whip sent erotic shivers up and down her spine.

Then, Jouet coiled it around Colette's wrists and forced her to parade around like a horse on a halter, before rubbing her breasts and sex with the bulbous handle and using the tip of the whip to tickle her anus. Then, Jouet gave her five lashes of the hair whip and then five more, each time striking her harder than the last. The stinging sensation of the human hair far surpassed the thwack of a paddle or the sting of a hand and soon Colette wanted to scream with enjoyment.

Next, he bound her in soft ropes and laid her on the floor. Colette peered up at her captor, adoringly. Today, at last, he'll beat my breasts and cunt she thought, as her pert nipples hardened with arousal.

Jouet rolled her onto her belly and beat her buttocks until they were raw and then he made her lie down and he fondled her, burying his face and cock in the luscious waves of her hair before he pushed his finger into her lubricious slit and began rubbing her clitoris. Colette was now experiencing such a burning sense of lust, she was crying out with excitement and her body was trembling with sexual frustration, as her greed for more spankilicious lashes of the whip grew and grew.

Jouet, who was dressed tonight in skin tight leather pants, loosened his zipper, and his penis which was swollen and pink and thickly veined, emerged like a serpent.

Colette shivered with delight as Jouet stood over her and began to flick the whip, her body giving little jerks as its tip struck first her breasts and her nipples. Jouet possessed an unerring accuracy. His life as a circus performer had given him such precision; he could touch any point on her body with a flick of his hand.

'Mark me,' Colette cried out as she tossed this way and that and her hips rose and fell as her orgasm began its incremental climb. 'I want the trophies of the spankilicious whip.'

'That's enough, get up, Colette. You're enjoying yourself far too much.'

Colette sat up pouting, but she knew better than to answer Jouet back. He'd only make her wait longer for her pleasure.

'Why won't you do it to me?' She cried, clambering onto her knees in front of Jouet. 'Beat me and make me come, I implore you. I can't stand it any more.'

Grasping Colette's hair tightly in his fist, Jouet stared into her eyes and then using the tip of the whip to lift Colette's hair, he curled a tress around it and tugged on it viciously.

'Stand up.' He reeled her in closer with the whip. 'Oh dear, your pretty hair's tangled in my hair whip, I shall have to make you loosen it. Un-knot your hair, Colette.'

'I can't,' Colette cried, as eyes watering she struggled to untangle the twisted strands and finally succeeded in freeing them.'

'Excite me and flatter me, Colette, and finally I shall give you what you want.' Colette sighed as she stared at Jouet's turgid cock. She didn't know which she now fancied inside her more, hot cock or hair whip.

'You must realise, no other man can wake the sex in me,

Jouet. Only your hair whip can unlock my sexuality, to the extent no other man has been able to. It's all I think about, day and night, and the only sexual satisfaction I get these days, is from perverted dreams about it. To be woven into the fabric of your life through the whip, is my only goal and I'd gladly sacrifice my hair for that.'

Jouet sensuously fingered the bulbous handle of the hair whip. 'If you're an exceptionally good and obedient girl and do exactly as I say, I think I'll beat you so hard you'll scream your desire. I might also lick it and make it nice and wet so it slides all the way into your tight cunt. OK, brush the tangles out of your hair and then I want you to cut it off as near as you can to the roots, so I have all of that luscious length.' Jouet tilted her chin this way and that. 'Actually, I think you'll look ultra-sexy with a short cut.'

Colette was trembling when Jouet returned with a pair of hairdressing scissors in his hand. 'I've waited ten years for a superb redhead, and as your reward I'll beat your cunt as red as your thatch. I confess my greatest weakness is for violent red hair and I fuck myself all night thinking about it.' Jouet suggestively rubbed his wet penis.

'Sit in front of the mirror, while I get off on watching you.'

Colette's legs were so weak she couldn't stand and Jouet had to help her to the chair. Finally, she brushed her hair until it shone and clutching the scissors and feeling her adrenaline surge, she snipped at it aggressively.

'Now, darling, bring the hair and come and kneel in front of me,' Jouet commanded.

Colette knelt before Jouet and held the hair out in her hands as she might an offering. Her misery at losing it was rapidly being eclipsed by the pleasurable sensation of her rising excitement.

'Colette, you may suck my tool and we'll finish the job. Firstly though, massage me with the hair.'

Colette massaged Jouet's penis with her hair, before

lowering her lips she eased the bulging shaft in her mouth and caressed it with her tongue from base to tip, as she cupped his balls.

'Now, lie down, Colette.'

Colette did so and Jouet spanked her on her tender little buttocks and then on her breasts as Colette wondered if at last this was the spankilicious finale she'd been dreaming of. With each strike of the whip the pain seemed to be eclipsed by wave after wave of scintillating intoxication.

'Open your legs as wide as they'll go, Colette.'

Colette did so and bit her lip as the tip of the whip parted her flaccid sex lips and moved up and down her sex slit and around her clitoris, before Jouet began to spank her.

Colette didn't scream, instead she smiled. She was experiencing delightful surges of emotion as her body dipped and soared in pre-orgasmic waves. However, she wasn't about to tell Jouet that. Oh no, she wanted more, and she knew the more she pleaded, the more thrills he would give her.

'Hit me harder, Jouet, it isn't hard enough,' she cried. 'Harder, harder.'

Strangely enough, on this occasion her orgasm still wouldn't come.

'Beat me on my cunt, Jouet,' she pleaded.

The strikes of the whip became a symphony of pain and pleasure.

'Hit me. It still isn't hard enough.' Colette's eyes glowed with perverse enjoyment as another strike bit into her tender sex.

'Come, you bitch,' Jouet groaned, as his fingers played over his distended penis. 'Isn't this enough for you? Most women would be in paroxysms of pleasure by now.'

'But I have an insatiable appetite, Jouet. You're not going to be the only man to fail to give me an orgasm, are you?'

Colette sighed in satisfaction, because inside she was

thinking, I shall need many more beatings with my own hair, before I reach the epitome of desire I wish to reach, and I'll make sure you indulge me in this particular fantasy, Jouet.

It's hard to know who holds the whip hand in any game of power play, but ultimately Colette knew she always gained the eventual advantage in any complex psychological battle.

This could be very interesting, very interesting indeed, she thought. I'm so aroused I feel reborn and having such long hair was after all, a damned nuisance. I much prefer this short cut.

'Hit me harder,' she cried, as she combed her fingers through her hair.

Just Watch Me
by Justine Elyot

Until last year, I hated having my photograph taken. In my graduation picture I have fringe in my eyes and I'm hugging a bag to my chest, as if in defence. Every school group or individual portrait features me looking off, slightly sideways, into the middle distance. Less formal studies taken on family holidays frequently feature the classic forearm-over-face pose. I couldn't even smile for a baby snap.

So my choice of recreational pursuit sometimes brings a wry grin to my face – not in mid-performance, of course, because I'm far too professional for that. But when I'm cleaning up my room, putting away the lube and the toys, or removing my lurid cosmetic veneer with a baby wipe, thoughts of the "funny old world" variety cross my mind. Then I switch off the webcam and log off, and I'm shy Sharleen again.

It was James who brought it out of me. I won't say he put the idea in my head, or changed my personality in some fundamental way, because I have always been an exhibitionist, I think. It's just that the urge was repressed for years and years, and it took some very skilful delving into my buried desires to spring it back out of its psychosexual jail.

James was the first boyfriend to talk dirty to me. I had always assumed that I would hate this kind of sex play, being a prim not-until-the-tenth-date kind of girl back then,

119

but my reaction to his nasty words shocked me deeply. It turned me on! Far from wanting to slide out from beneath him and deal a ladylike slap to his roguish cheek, I just wanted to spread my legs wider, throw my head further back and beg to be told again that I was a bitch in heat who needed cock morning, noon and night.

'You can't get enough, can you, Shar?'

'No, no, more, more.'

'You're going to get more. As much as I can give you. And then I'm going to call my friends and have them come and fuck you too.'

I moaned luxuriously. I knew he wasn't serious, but the *thought* of him seeing me as a girl who would do that was just explosively hot. I imagined myself, taking cock after cock, while his friends (in untucked plaid shirts and two-day stubble) cheered and raised cans of beer to each performer in turn.

The fantasy was broadened and extended every time we fucked, new details being added or experimented with as James worked on discovering exactly what pushed my buttons the hardest and quickest. He was good. Within a few weeks, he had perfected the script, and brought me out of my hiding place and into the golden sun of sexual freedom. I trusted him enough to show him all that I was, even the bits that seemed reprehensible or dangerous, and the high-wire thrill of it kept me buzzing day and night.

'What if we did it for real?' he asked one night, after exhausting energetic sex all over the living room and hallway, with the curtains not completely closed.

'Did *what* for real?' I yawned, examining my knees for carpet burn. Ouch. Yep.

'Had a third party over … just to watch. Or to … join in.'

My eyes flew wide open. 'I don't know,' I said. 'Are you serious?'

'I just think … it would add something. If it was someone we both knew … and trusted. It could be quite hot. Don't you think? I mean, not if you don't want to, of course!'

'Male or female?'

'Either. Your choice. Both, if you want.' He grinned. 'Or neither. Anyway, it's just a thought.' He sounded agitated now, as if worried that he had gone too far and expected me to run for the hills. 'No biggie. Not a deal breaker or anything.'

'You're a pervert,' I said.

'Well, yeah,' he said, in a "duh!" kind of way.

'But,' I said thoughtfully, laying my head back in his lap, 'so am I.'

In the end, we went for Craig, James' flatmate. He had already heard our extravagant bedroom symphonies and, rather than turn up the sound on the TV to drown out our voices and creaking bedsprings, he apparently liked to put a glass to the wall and listen in. Halfway to voyeur already – he seemed the ideal candidate.

James got me hot and bothered while we waited for Craig to come home from work by telling me about the conversations they had had about me over pints in the local pub. 'He knows what you're like,' James told me, sitting me on his lap and snogging me hard, curtains wide, one hand up my top. 'I've told him that you like it hard and often. I've told him about your sweet, tight cunt and your round, red nipples. I've told him that I've fucked your arse and you loved it. He knows you're a dirty slut and he can't wait to see it for himself.'

'God.' I was gulping, throat dry, knickers soaked. 'Are we really doing this?'

'Relax, babe. If you don't want to do anything, just say the word. He's only going to watch, though.'

His key turned in the lock and I hid in James' resumed kiss, letting him put his hand up my skirt, baring my thigh to the eye of the newcomer, who had thrown his bags down in the hall and was home. Home and hungry.

'Well, well.' His voice was a little unsteady, trying too

hard for detached amusement. 'What have we here? James and Shar sitting in a tree K.I.S.S.I.N.G. Please don't mind me – carry on.'

So we did. Carried on clinching on the sofa until my top was off and my skirt down.

'What do you think, Craig?' James broke off from sucking my nipple to throw the question over to the armchair. I looked over at him; he had released his cock and held it in a fierce fist. His face was pink all over, and looked bloated, his eyes reduced to piggy slits of lust.

There were two ways I could go now. I could shake myself out of this madness and bolt from the room, clutching skirt and top. James was a decent sort of bloke – he wouldn't hold it against me. Or I could do what I did – move one of my hands down inside my knickers, holding Craig's eyes all the while, and splay my fingertips across my wet vulva, ready to thrum in a slow, steady kind of way, for the benefit of a stranger.

'You're not shy, are you?' said Craig, trying to keep the tone light, but sounding like a buffoon instead, like the probably-virginal techno-geek that he was. Poor Craig. I felt a little sorry for him. This was strong stuff for an introduction to the thrills of voyeurism. But I was past shame now, past modesty, well past my old-fashioned cast-off morality.

'Actually,' I panted, letting James remove the knickers and bra entirely. 'I am. This seems to be ... an anomaly ...'

It came out something like "ammamolomoly" though, because James' tongue had come to land on my clit and I could no longer say long or complicated words.

'Oh my God!' whimpered Craig, crouching down to crotch level for a better view. His spectacle lenses steamed up and I came, for the first time of many, thrusting my hips right at him, right at his face.

He did nothing but watch, that first time. There were subsequent occasions, but he never wanted to join in, and that was fine with me. His bottle-lensed, bug-eyed gaze was good enough for me; enough to take me where I wanted to go.

But Craig got promoted and moved away, and James and I lost our audience. We moved on to dogging, which was interesting, but somehow I could not shake the anxiety that our audience might lose control and harm us, or rob us. I wanted to show myself off in a safe space, it seemed.

Then James came up with what seemed like a perfect solution.

'Webcam,' he said, producing a little metal eye from his coat pocket as we sat in the local pub after work.

'What, like on Skype?'

'Yeah. Except we could do a live streaming website. Or perhaps just make a couple of clips first, until you're confident with live stuff. What do you think?'

'Clips?'

'Yeah. Put them on one of those porny versions of YouTube. See how many people bite. Invite them to come and sign up for a live streaming site. We could even make money from it!'

'I don't want to make money from it. I wouldn't have a clue how to declare it on my tax return.'

'Even better! We'll get loads of punters if they know it's free. Just think, Shar, you could have thousands of men getting off on watching you get fucked – all at the same time. What a head trip!'

'Yes,' I echoed. 'What a head trip.'

Initially, I took some persuading. 'What if I was seen by someone I knew?'

'You can wear a mask, or we can pixellate your face.'

'I want them to see my face when I come, though.'

'Perhaps we can have a Valued Customer programme – the ones who stay on, who we learn we can trust, get to see your face.'

'Maybe.'

'We do it the way you want it, Shar. It's your site. We can be as wild, or as tame, as you like.'

James was in IT, so he knew his way around a few lines of code. He designed a website that was as tackily glamorous as I envisaged, then he got Craig to come down for the weekend and film us on a marathon session, which he cut up into five minute clips and placed on PerveNet.

It was a different kind of thrill, watching my luminous eyes and my grainy body on a snippet of film anyone could watch. The statistics mounted quickly; within a couple of days, thousands of people had watched me spread my legs and make myself come with a vibrator, or seen James fuck me from behind while I hid my face in a pillow. Messages piled up beneath the clips, indicating that there was substantial interest in seeing more of me. 'I WILL PAY TO WATCH U FUCK HER GOOD, DUDE' said sk8rboiNJ, while LetMeWatch69 suggested 'I BET SHE LOVES IT'. Every little comment was like an expulsion of hot breath on my clit; a glimpse into the lust-glazed eyes of an aircraft-hangar full of voyeurs. I imagined them, all standing together, a seething mass of teeth-bared carnality, all focused on my split thighs and open pussy. I liked it.

The site has been live for over two years now, and we have close to 10,000 members. That is 10,000 cocks – and perhaps the odd pussy – being taken in hand along with my thrice-weekly Performance Hour.

I love my work, and I am constantly devising new, fresh and surprising elements to add to all the fantasy staples. Sometimes I go solo, with toys, or just a slow sexy striptease and masturbation scene. More often, James joins in and we will have an enthusiastic, no-holds-barred fuck to camera, watching the comments and messages roll in as we roll all over the bed. Once a month, I do a "request show", where I take a few viewers' favourite fantasies and give them a bespoke re-enactment.

Today's presentation is a completely new spin, though,

and I must admit I am nervous. For the first time, I am running a competition. And the first prize is … me.

The competition winner, having been vetted and interviewed by James, but not yet seen by me, is waiting in the living room while I prepare for tonight's eagerly-anticipated broadcast. The idea is that I wrap myself from head to toe in metallic red wrapping paper, finishing off with a huge rosette at my crotch. I look quite fetching, in a strange way, I decide, posing in front of my dresser mirror. I have wound tight strips of the foil-wrapping up each leg and arm and around my torso, sellotaping it in strategic places. Despite the head-to-toe coverage, a person would only have to take hold of the top ribbon at my collarbone and pull for it all to rip in half and fall to the floor.

No mask tonight, or blindfold – the viewing public is made up of our 500 "VoyeurPlus" membership, all of whom have become quite "well known" to us over the course of the site's life, so I need not worry about local boys or stray uncles logging on. I switch on the cam and open for business, shaking with nerves at having to perform the one part of this role that genuinely frightens me – speaking to camera. Usually James does it, but tonight he has a different function, and I must speak the words, trying to sound cheeky and confident while the back of my throat dries and my hands tremble. At least they can't see the blush, as red as my wrapping, suffusing my throat and collarbone beneath the layers of foil paper.

'Good evening, one and all,' I quaver, keeping my body in motion, twirling and flexing, to distract me from the hideous sounds coming out of my mouth. 'As you know, you are here to witness a brand new development on the site – one which we hope will be a success, and can be repeated. Yes, tonight I get fucked by the winner of our recent competition – Mr Pussywatch, as he is known to us, had managed to total the most viewing hours of any member in the past year, so tonight he gets to sample a little bit of what he has seen. Gosh, I'm looking forward to it, and I hope you are too. Remember, keep watching, and it might be you here next time.' I rub the rosette at my crotch, enjoying the rustle, enjoying the thought of all those cocks stiffening to attention despite my nerves.

A few comments are coming in already. 'YOU HAVE A SWEET LITTLE VOICE – YOU SHOULD SPEAK MORE OFTEN'. 'ARE YOU NERVOUS? YOU SOUND NERVOUS.' 'YR HANDS ARE SHAKING – IS YR PUSSY WET YET?'

I turn away from the screen and call down through the half-open bedroom door. 'Are you ready, guys?'

I hear the double footfall on the stairs, and I laid myself down on the bed, ribbon tied, soon to be unwrapped, awaiting my fate.

James enters first, video camera in hand, for he intends to film our scene from several different angles in order to edit a more explicit and interesting film from the crude web footage – hopefully we will be able to sell it. Then, Mr Pussywatch (real name, Steven) slips into the room and I get my first glimpse. He is in his late 20s, with short cropped dirty-blond hair and a grittily attractive face. I have been very lucky, I realise, although part of the perverse thrill for me had been the idea that I might have landed somebody deeply unattractive, or just a bit creepy-looking, like Craig. Steve hooks his thumbs into the belt of his jeans and stares down at me from transparent bluish eyes. He has thick lips and they curl up into a slightly sneery smile.

'Best present I've had all year,' he remarks to James. 'I know what's inside though. Spoils the surprise a bit.'

James chuckles. 'You won't be disappointed, mate. I promise you.' The camera light changes from red to green. Action. 'Go and unwrap her. She's all yours.'

Steven approaches quite slowly, as if he can't quite make up his mind whether I'm real or illusory. When he reaches the side of the bed, he puts out a hand – a large, callused, workman's hand – and lays it on the tight-wrapped slope of a breast. I like the weight of him, and I let myself shimmy slightly, rustling beneath his touch.

'You up for it, Starleen?' he asks. Starleen is my Camgirl name.

'I'm always up for it,' I tell him.

He likes my answer, and kneels down on the bed, laying hands everywhere now, finishing with the big rosette between my thighs.

'I want to see you,' he says. 'And so do the rest of the boys. Let's take this off.' He tucks a finger inside the top ribbon, running from shoulder to shoulder, and jerks sharply downward. The sellotape warps before falling away, allowing the paper to rip with a satisfying sweep from top to bottom, twirls of paper tickling my body and flying across the room. It is the work of avid seconds to bare me from neck to toe, though he seems to want to keep the few strips that vaguely cross my eyes and lips, loosely enough that I can see and talk, but just giving the decorative effect of gagging and blindfolding.

Steve stays on one side of me, conscious of how the camera angle works, presenting my nakedness to the viewers with a sweep of his meaty hands.

'Look at this,' he says, seeming to enjoy his moment of notoriety. 'What a treat. I tell you what, guys; the camera doesn't really do her justice. She is good enough to eat.' He squeezes my tits, watching the nipples pop up above his fists, all hard and cherry red. 'In fact, I might just do that.' His mouth is on the stiff buds, licking and slavering, making sure that the cam picks up the tip of his tongue plastering and coating them. The sensitive nerve endings go wild, sending rapid pulses down to my pussy, causing it to contract and flood with juices. And his hand is there now, discovering the evidence. He pushes one thigh, making sure my lips are split wide and fully visible to my audience. 'Camera doesn't always pick up how wet and juicy she is,' he gasps, lifting his teeth from one nipple to gasp into the unswerving digital eye that watches us. 'But take it from me, she is as fucking wet as … as …' His powers of simile elude him, and he contents himself with pushing broad fingers up inside me, enjoying the sounds and sensations, while he bends his head and devours my tits again. I can feel his erection hard up against my hip now, pushing at the rough denim that restrains it.

'Is this good, darlin'?' he wants to know, nuzzling my neck as his fingers spear me. 'I've seen you do yourself so many times … I can't believe I'm fingering this pussy I've watched three times a week for two years … and soon I'm going to be fucking it.' He nips my earlobe and I moan. James is crouching down at the foot of the bed, getting an unrestricted view of my spread legs and Steven's thumb rubbing my clit.

'I'm going to come,' I warn them, and James scuttles up to film my ribbony face, mouth open, puffing and blowing, while Steven takes a whole breast in his mouth and keeps the finger-pressure up, up, up until I've committed my orgasm to posterity.

Through blurred, tired eyes, I can see the comments rolling in. 'HOT HOT HOT!' 'WHAT YOU WAITING FOR? FUCK HER!' 'SHE IS LOVING THIS!'

I find myself arse-to-camera, thighs wide, head down while he whips off his clothes. James, to fill the brief time this takes, uses his camera-free hand to stroke and caress my bum, running his hand down my cheeks, then my cleft, to my soaked pussy, just to keep a bit of interest for the audience.

'How are you having her, mate?' he asks Steven conversationally. 'Doggy style always looks good in profile.'

'Yeah, that'll do,' he grunts, bent on action now rather than dialogue. I crawl around to present a side-on aspect, keeping my head low and my bottom high while Steven snaps on a rubber. As he penetrates and fucks me, I imagine – as I always do – what the viewers are seeing. They don't see the headboard, jerking a little with each hard thrust, as I do. They see a hard, thick cock, shiny with my juices, slipping back and forth inside me. They see my stretched lips and his big hands on my hips. They see my shocked face and his determined jaw. They even see James, half-lying on the floor to try and get the most obscene shot he possibly can, pointing his lens up at my filled pussy.

'You are fucking her good,' he says, his voice treacly-thick, the way it is when he is trying to fight lust. He will want his turn soon, I think with a thrill, and I push myself back on Steven's rod, circling my hips, inviting him deeper still.

Steve slams a big palm down on my backside when he comes, which hurts a bit, but at least he is gentleman enough to wait for my own climax before he succumbs to his, which I always appreciate. James catches a close-up of the big red handprint on my rear cheek. 'Oh, I'm going to get a still of *that*,' he crows. 'Screencap of the night, I think.'

I am still recovering from Steven's firm handling of me when James hands the camera over to the competition winner, unzips his trousers and poses me on my knees on the bed for a blow job. I try to catch my breath around his cock, hearing Steve crack open a restorative beer over on the wicker bedroom chair, and wiggle my arse for the camera. What a show they are getting tonight. I feel proud, and urge myself on to deliver the performance of my lifetime, licking my lips and taking James' cock as deep as I can, sucking and squeezing his balls while the corner of my eye strays to the screen.

'DIRTY BITCH – WHY DON'T I KNOW A GIRL LIKE HER?' 'WHEN'S THE NEXT COMP?' 'WHERE IS THE OTHER BLOKE?'

Swiftly, James releases my mouth and spins me round to face the corner where Steve sits with the camera in one hand

and his rapidly tumescing cock in the other.

'Fancy another round?' asks my James. 'Come and sit her on your prick while I put the camera on the tripod. Feel like I have to have her arse, but I can't do it and film it at the same time.'

Steve doesn't need to be told twice; he leaps back on to the bed and manhandles me over his upright cock, plunging me down and clamping an arm around my back so that my breasts press into his chest and my face is snug in the hollow of his shoulder. It feels delicious; rude and satisfying, and the additional element of my open bottom cheeks, expectant of imminent attention, is sinfully piquant. James is soon at our rear, spreading me wide, lubing me up, and then he eases in, talking to camera in his expert way.

'See how I'm gliding in … quite slowly … just filling her up without rushing … and she doesn't even try to resist … cos she loves this … don't you, Star? You love it up the arse … and now you're getting it with a cock in your pussy too … of course, she's had it with a dildo up there before … but never a real-live cock … how do you like it, Star? I think our audience would like to know …'

Our audience will have to interpret my incoherent groans, though, because I am far beyond forming words now. I am Star. I am a star. I am watched, fucked, buggered, brought to my limit and held there, for all to see. I let them take me, both ways, all ways, until my bones give way and I become pure sensation, pure flesh and sex, captured on film for all time.

The first thing I see when I emerge from the fog of multiple orgasms is a gigantic comment rolling across the screen.

'YOU'VE COME A LONG WAY, BABY. KEEP ON COMING! LOVE, CRAIG.'

Jillaroo for a Week
by Eva Hore

We were backpacking around Australia and having the most amazing time. We'd met up with some fantastic people along the way, hopefully making lifelong friends in the process. A girl from Sweden, Anna, gave us an address to be a Jillaroo for a week. Jillaroo was a name the Aussies used for cowgirl. You got to work on the ranch, free board and lodgings and $1,000 per week to boot. She said most of the employees were girls and she had some nights there of wild passion. Sounded just up our alley.

I couldn't wait to get there. The thought of spreading my thighs across a galloping stallion, girls in tight jeans and leather chaps, earthy smells and outdoor campfires certainly had my juices flowing, so we decided why not. We were always up for new adventures.

A farmer drove us out to the property in his old and beaten down Ute. We were overawed with the size of the homestead. Their land went for miles. Beautifully painted white fences boarded out the different paddocks, some had sheep and cattle grazing, the others were planted with crops and near the home were Arabian stallions prancing around, snorting and kicking up their hind legs as thunder rolled around the hills.

'Here you go, girls,' the farmer said stopping at the end of the long and dusty driveway. 'You just go up and knock on the front door. Tell them Ned said to say hi.'

Jumping out of the back of the Ute we thanked him

profusely and headed up the porch steps. Just as we were about to knock, the door opened and a beautiful black girl stood there in the doorway.

She was gorgeous. Large brown eyes, thick black hair, voluptuous tits that spilled out of her skimpy top and she was wearing a pair of skin tight shorts, so tight that you actually could see the parting of her pussy lips. It took me a minute to find my voice.

'Hi, I'm Melissa,' I said, 'and this is my friend, Sheila.'

'Hello,' she said smiling.

'We're here to see Jock?'

She nodded and sauntered off. As she turned I saw that her shorts were halfway up the crack of her arse, her cheeks plump and firm, just begging to be touched. We stood there waiting. An old aboriginal woman wearing a checked apron opened the door wide.

'Come on in, girls,' she said. 'Good to see you made it here in one piece.'

'Thanks,' we said as we stood in the grand foyer. The house was enormous; a huge staircase sweeping up in an arc to the top floor took up most of the foyer. At the top of the stairs the most stunningly beautiful-looking woman I've ever seen stood peering down at us. She was wearing a tight pair of jeans, skin tight singlet and riding boots.

She quickly descended, held out her hand for us to shake.

'I'm Nicky,' she said. 'Welcome. My dad's not here at the moment, he's out mustering.'

We introduced ourselves and she took us for a tour of the property.

Walking up towards the converted shearing sheds she pointed out things of interest for us.

'The men's quarters are down there. I usually keep them separated from us girls. I've had some trouble with a few of them so they know not to cross me any more or they're out. Just keep your distance from them and you'll be fine. Anna tell you much about what we do here?'

'Just that we have to help out with mustering and keep the stables in order,' I said.

'That's right. It's all pretty simple. You can both ride can't you?'

'Yeah, we were in pony club back home,' Sheila said, eyeing Nicky's arse as she walked briskly in front of us.

The stables were not far from the shearing shed. We had to share with four other girls who were out at the moment on an adjoining property with her dad doing the mustering. They wouldn't be back until the day after tomorrow, Nicky said.

'Dinner is in ten minutes, so if you want to freshen up, the bathrooms are through that door,' she said, pointing the way. 'Just go to the back of the house and in through to the kitchen.

'Thanks,' I said.

'Just settle in tonight and tomorrow I'll give you your chores.' She smiled and walked off leaving us to ourselves.

'She's gorgeous,' Sheila said.

'I know. Did you check out her arse in those jeans? And her tits, man would I love to suck on them.'

'God, I'd love to see her naked in the showers. I can't believe they pay $1,000 for all this. Everything seems in order, what on earth are we going to do all day?'

'Beats me, come on,' I said, 'let's go eat and then while there's a bit of daylight left we can go for a bit of walk.'

The aboriginal woman, Martha, gave us a nice stew and some homemade bread. We insisted on doing the dishes and she showed us her appreciation by giving us a bottle of her home brewed beer. There was a small kitchenette in our quarters so we popped it in the fridge to chill.

We unpacked quickly and went exploring. The countryside was breathtaking. Tall majestic gum trees swayed as the wind rushed through them. Eucalyptus gums had the whole area smelling delightful, and the hint of rain in the air had my senses reeling. High up in one of the branches we spotted our first koala. We were so excited that we hadn't realised how close to the men's quarters we'd gone. Hiding behind some thick bushes we waited until the coast was clear before making our way to one of the windows.

There were only a few guys in there playing cards. They looked harmless enough and as the darkness of night descended we made our way back, intending to skirt around the stables. The neighing of the horses drew our attention and what sounded like the cracking of a whip had us sneaking down around the back.

It was very dark. Hiding in the shadows we peeked around the door of the stable. A light shone from beneath a doorway. It must have been the tack room. Angry voices filtered through. Being nosey by nature, we made our way around to the outside and found the window. An old curtain was pulled across the glass. Intrigued as to who would be in there, I found an old crate and hoisted myself up.

What I saw certainly shocked me.

I could see that Nicky was inside with Martha. Martha was smacking a whip into the open palm of her hand. They seemed to be arguing but I couldn't make out what they were saying.

'What's going on?' Sheila whispered.

'Shh,' I said. 'Hang on.'

'You were out there with the men, weren't you?' Martha said.

'No, er, I was just …'

'You were just what? As soon as your father's not here you go looking for trouble. Now I told your dad I'd look after you like my own and I think you need to be punished.'

'But I didn't do anything.'

'But you were going to weren't you?'

'I … er …' she mumbled.

'Get those clothes off,' Martha demanded.

I nearly fell off the crate when I heard that. I indicated for

Sheila to give me her hand and we both balanced precariously on it as we watched Nicky remove her clothing. Her figure was even better than I'd thought. As she peeled her panties down and stood in front of Martha naked my pussy began to throb.

'What are they doing?' Sheila whispered.

'Shh,' I said.

Martha grabbed her by the arm and pushed her towards a post that was holding up the ceiling. She put her back hard up against it and took a rope that was lying on the table and threaded it around Nicky's wrists. Then she took a chair, pulled it in next to the post for her to stand on and hooked the rope around a large nail that had been hammered in there.

With her arms straining upwards, her gorgeous breasts were lifted high, the nipples erect and inviting. She had a gorgeous bush of pubic hair and long sexy legs. Martha went and got the whip and began to flick it around the room. Nicky flinched every time it cracked the air.

'You think I should give you some lashings?' Martha said.

'No,' Nicky whispered, acting as though she were frightened, although I doubted that very much by the way she licked her lips.

She slapped at her breasts with her open palm. I watched spellbound as they swayed and jiggled under Martha's hand. 'You think I should give you a few more of these?'

She said nothing. Just stood there mute.

Martha took the handle end of the whip and wiggled it in between her thighs.

'Open your legs,' she demanded.

Nicky obeyed and Martha rubbed the handle along her slit.

'Open them wider,' Martha demanded.

She did and Martha fell to her knees before her, her dark fingers opening up her pussy lips as Nicky opened her legs

135

even wider. Sheila and I were mesmerized by what was unfolding before us. Martha's head was getting closer and closer to Nicky's pussy. Her tongue stretched forward to lick at her. Nicky thrust her pelvis forward, begging for Martha to give her pussy a good licking.

'Is this what you wanted the men to do to you?' Martha mumbled.

Nicky's head fell back, 'Hmm,' was all she said.

'You wanted them to stick their tongues in your cunt, didn't you? Like this,' she said.

My pussy was getting wetter by the second. I wanted nothing more than to be in Martha's place right now. Who would have thought that Nicky would have allowed herself to be strung up like that? She was obviously into some kinky shit and I was hoping that before this week was over that we'd see more of it, perhaps even participate in some.

'Or maybe you wanted them to stick their cocks in your cunt and fuck you, like this?'

Still on her knees she rammed the handle of the whip into her pussy, pushing it up and down. I could see her juices glistening on the dark handle and then Martha lifted Nicky's leg and threw it over her shoulder. Her pussy was gaping wide open and now Martha was inserting her black fingers into Nicky's white cunt.

I was fascinated by the colour contrast. I'd never made love to a dark woman and even though Martha wasn't my type, the thought of her fat tongue lapping at my pussy, or her thick fingers probing my cunt, had my juices flowing. I was hoping it was having the same effect on Sheila.

The rain that had been threatening to fall did so just then. Heavy splats of rain fell upon us. Sheila and I scampered off the crate and ran back to our quarters, shaking off the drops of rain.

'Wow, can you believe that,' Sheila said.

'I know. Let's get out of these wet clothes,' I said.

We stripped off and pulled on our baggy tracksuits,

sitting cross legged on the beds.

'I wonder what else they're doing down there?' I said, conscious of the way my own pussy was gaping open as we sat on the beds.

'Probably giving her a really good licking, I'd say.'

'Do you want to go back?'

'You're kidding,' Sheila said.

'Nope. We can throw on our raincoats. I'm dying to know.'

'OK,' Sheila said, grabbing hers and throwing me mine.

We ran quickly and lightly back to the window. Nicky was lying across the table now, her long blonde hair cascading down to fall off the edge. Her feet had been placed firmly on the table and her legs were dropped open so her pussy was yawning at us. Splayed out like that she looked magnificent. It took all my willpower not to rush in and devour her pussy. The rain began to beat down faster but I didn't even notice. I was so focused on the activities in the tack room.

'Martha had the whip in her hand and began to lightly whip Nicky's pussy. Nicky's knees half closed every time and every time Martha just smacked them open again. On the floor was a small box and I watched Martha reach down and pull out some pegs. She opened one up and pinched it down on Nicky's nipple. Nicky cried out and it looked as though it hurt her but as Martha placed another on her other nipple Nicky tweaked them, enjoying the pain it would have been giving her.

Now Martha placed pegs on her outer pussy lips. Tugging at them she opened her up wide and buried her head between Nicky's open thighs.

'Oh yeah,' Nicky said. 'Oh yeah. Lick it, lick it hard.'

Martha was nuzzling in, licking, lapping, kissing. She was really burrowing in and Nicky's thighs closed around her fuzzy dark hair. The contrast of her dark skin and hair buried deep into Nicky's white, creamy body was too much

137

for me. I grabbed Sheila's hand and pulled her off the crate. We ran back to our rooms and tore off our raincoats.

'Fuck,' I said. 'I haven't felt this horny for ages.'

'Me too,' Sheila said pulling my T-shirt over my head before taking off her own.

I lay on the bed and Sheila straddled my head. As she lowered her pussy down towards my eager mouth I could only think of Nicky. I wondered what her scent would be like, what she'd taste like and how wonderful it would be to have her between my legs right now.

Don't get me wrong. Sheila and I had a great relationship. We were best friends and sometimes great lovers. We grew up together and have shared many things, our bodies included. We weren't madly in love with each other. We respected each other and at times like these it was nothing for us to get each other off until the real thing came along.

Devouring her pussy I allowed my tongue ring to slide over her clit. She reciprocated by smearing my clit with saliva before finding the very centre of my nub and rubbing in circular motions. We both knew what the other needed and it wasn't long before we were coming. Later, we lay together on my bed, staring up at the ceiling.

'That was great,' she said tweaking my nipple.

'Hmm. I wonder what the other girls are like.'

'I wonder if Nicky's father knows what's going on when he's not here?'

'Don't know but I'm hoping we get to see a lot more of Nicky and Martha. Next time what do you say we join in?'

'I don't know.'

'Come on. What can they do? Sack us? Who cares, we're the ones on holiday. We'll just pack up and go elsewhere. What do you say?'

'Yeah, OK,' she giggled. 'I'm game if you are.'

We eventually fell asleep and fortunately the ringing of a bell woke us, as we were both naked, our arms and legs

138

tangled together. We rose and quickly dressed and made our way down to the kitchen for breakfast.

'Morning,' I said when I saw Martha serving Nicky's breakfast, as though last night had never happened.

'Morning, girls,' Martha said. 'Did you sleep well?'

'Like a baby,' I said.

'When you've finished we'll saddle up some horses and take supplies out to the others.'

'How much longer will they be out there?' Martha asked.

'Knowing Dad, probably two more days I'd say,' Nicky said.

After saddling up the horses we strapped on the supplies and headed off. I wondered what the guys would be doing today. Apart from spying on them while they played cards, we hadn't seen them again and they certainly weren't around this morning.

It was great riding through the paddocks, my thighs spread across the back of this massive beast. I loved riding horses, like most girls. The pressure on my clit was fantastic, especially after last night's activities. I was still swollen and the pressure was exquisite. I could do it all day, but unfortunately we finally came across the others.

Man, Nicky's father was drop dead gorgeous. If I was straight I'd jump him straight away. Nicky introduced us to everyone and we joined them all for lunch. There were cattle around, but I didn't see any branding tools which is what I assumed they'd be doing. There were deckchairs and recliners near their tents and they had a big wagon with them. I wondered what they had inside it.

There were only three girls here. I wondered where the other one was. All the girls were gorgeous. Their jeans skin tight, their breasts straining to burst from their tight shirts and I noticed they all wore make-up. Something seemed a bit fishy. I would have loved to come back out here tonight and do some spying. I bet there'd be lots of action going on with Jock. I looked at him harder. Was he wearing make-up?

Later, while Nicky spoke in private with her father, I tried to make conversation with one of the girls called Sue.

'So, have you done much branding?' I asked.

'What?' She giggled.

'Aren't you guys branding out here?'

'Oh yeah, sorry I didn't quite understand.'

'What else have you been doing?'

'Huh? Oh, nothing much, just hanging with the cattle,' she said giggling.

She was hiding something, I knew that. I looked over at the others. They were all wearing make-up and I didn't see anything that would indicate that they were out here working with the cattle. Before I had a chance to ask more, Nicky came back and we saddled up and rode back.

'Feel like a dip?' Nicky yelled out as we cantered through a river.

'Yeah, why not,' I said, giving Sheila the nod.

Climbing down off our horses, we let them graze while we took off our clothing. I had intended to leave my underwear on, but Nicky stripped right off and jumped in. Sheila and I looked at each other and thought, why not, so we did too.

'Isn't this great?' Nicky gushed.

'It's fucking freezing,' Sheila said, getting out.

Nicky just laughed and splashed water at Sheila's white arse as she climbed up the embankment.

'What about you?'

'Me, I'm fine,' I said, as she dived underwater.

I gasped as her fingers tugged at my inner thighs. I parted them with her insistence and she wiggled between them. She came up laughing and spluttering. She was one weird and unusual woman I can tell you. We played around for a bit before dragging ourselves out. Sheila was sitting on her shirt allowing the sun to dry off her body.

'You've got a great figure,' Nicky said to Sheila.

'Thanks,' Sheila said blushing.

Nicky flopped on her own shirt next to Sheila and they began talking about our travels. It was the weirdest thing to be lying naked out in the Australian outback, talking about our adventures as though it was the most normal thing in the world. I must admit I was a bit jealous as I rather fancied Nicky myself.

Before long we dressed and made our way back. Nicky left us to unsaddle the horses and rub them down and then we were to muck out the stables.

'What the fuck were you two talking about?' I asked Sheila.

'Nothing much,' she said, smirking at me. 'Not jealous are you?'

The bitch, she knew me well.

'This place is weird,' I said.

'Yeah, I know.'

'Did you notice all the girls were wearing make-up?'

'Yeah, and so was her dad.'

'I know. I didn't see any branding stuff, did you?'

'Nope,' I said, shovelling up horse shit and throwing it into a bin.

'And what about those guys last night? Have you seen them anywhere?'

'No, I haven't.'

'I reckon they're into something.'

'Like what?'

'Movies. I reckon they're making their own porno.'

'No way,' Sheila laughed.

'OK, tonight after dinner, let's do some more sneaking around. I want to go down where the guys are and see what they're up to. You can't tell me they just sit around playing cards all day and night.'

We finished off the day by tilling up some earth in the veggie patch before spreading out compost. We were both filthy and in dire need of a bath. There were two baths and two showers in the bathroom so we filled up both baths and dropped in some bath salts.

Relaxing back I thought about the skinny dipping with Nicky. She'd grazed the inside of my thighs and touched my pussy lips a few times when she was making her way through my thighs. Me, I didn't dare touch her. Although I wanted to. I wished we'd been in a pool so I could have seen her pussy up close but the water in the river was murky so I saw nothing.

I was jealous when she gave Sheila all her attention when we got out. What game was she playing at? Coming on to me and then Sheila. I was lying there thinking that we should be on guard here, after all we were a long way from town, when Sheila startled me.

'Did you hear that?' she said.

'What?'

'That noise. It sounded like someone was outside the window.'

I peered over and saw no one. The curtains hadn't been drawn tightly and there was a gap. She jumped out of the bath and quickly opened them. She looked gorgeous, standing there with soapy suds dripping off her nude body.

'Well?'

'Nothing, but I was sure I heard something.'

'That's just your guilty conscience from last night,' I said, rising and drying myself off. 'Let's go down for dinner. I'm starved.'

When we knocked lightly on the kitchen door before entering I saw the dark girl who had opened the door for us yesterday.

'Hello,' I said. 'What's your name?'

'Margarita,' she said.

'Where's Martha?' I asked.

'I'm here,' Martha said, coming back into the room. 'Go and help Nicky.'

Margarita scampered off and Martha looked as though

she was cross. We ate in silence, did the dishes again and then left. Sheila wanted to look through the windows and see where Nicky was and what she was doing. I thought we should get as far away as possible. I was more than eager to see what the guys were up to tonight.

We stayed in our room until nine p.m. It was pitch black by then and we had trouble finding our way over the paddocks. Climbing over the railing fence we snuck closer, the light from their window leading the way for us.

'Fuck,' I heard a guy say. 'She's got great tits.'

'Look at her pussy. Wouldn't you like to get your tongue in that?' another voice said.

'Oh yeah. Check out her arse. Bet she's never had a cock up there,' one laughed.

Trying not to giggle we peered in the window. It was obvious they were watching porn. They were sprawled out in a lounge area. The television was on, but we couldn't see what they were watching but could certainly see that they were naked and all had erections.

Two were stroking their own cocks. I pulled back and so did Sheila.

'Fucking hell,' I said. 'Let's get out of here.'

We made to go back, but then I heard my own voice. It was coming from the television. How could that be? They were watching porn, weren't they? Alarmed, we scurried around the other side and peeked in through another window. They were watching Sheila and me making love from last night. Somehow they'd taped us. There must have been a camera set up in our room and they'd video taped it all.

Sheila's eyes were glued to the set. I nudged her, indicating I wanted her to follow me back. But where were we safe from prying eyes? What else did they have bugged? I didn't have a clue. All I knew was I had to get that tape and destroy it, but how?

We sat in deep grass, the twinkling of stars our only light.

Our eyes became accustomed to the darkness and we could see fairly well.

'What do we do now?' Sheila asked.

'We wait until they've gone to bed and then we sneak in and get the tape.'

'No way,' she said. 'What if they wake up?'

'We make a run for it.'

'Run where?'

'Shit, I don't know.'

We'd never been in a situation like this before. If we managed to get the tape, how would we get off the property? We'd arranged with the guy who'd dropped us off to pick us up in seven days. How would we get to the nearest town and which direction was it in? Those noises outside the bathroom window? Did these guys tape us in the bath too or were they just spying on us. This was not how I envisaged a week as a Jillaroo, I can tell you.

Finally at 3.30 a.m. the lights went off. We waited another half hour before trying their door. I was surprised and pleased it was unlocked and I tiptoed into the lounge, while Sheila stood guard. To my delight, I saw that the tape was still in the VCR. Pressing the eject button it slid out quietly, and, holding my breath I made my way back out the door.

Holding the tape close to my chest we ran back to our room. Just before entering though I pulled Sheila back.

'They might be watching us now. We can't take the tape in there.'

'What are we going to do?'

'We'll have to bury it.'

'Where?'

'How the fuck do I know? Anywhere. We'll have to tell them in the morning that you got a call on your mobile that your dad is sick and we have to go home. See if Nicky can take us back to town before the guys wake up and realise it's gone.'

'Yeah, that's good. Good idea.'

'Come on. Let's go further out, bury this where no one will think of looking.'

We found a spot and buried it, throwing gum leaves and composted dirt over it, hoping no one would stumble upon it. Before we buried it we also pulled out the ribbon, hoping in doing that, that we'd destroyed the images. What a nightmare!

Neither of us spoke all the way back to our room. We lay in bed feigning sleep, just in case and I set the alarm to go off early. We packed quickly, took everything with us and waited for the kitchen lights to come on, before rushing down to see Martha.

Babbling like idiots we explained about Sheila's dad. Martha fortunately believed us and without hesitation she grabbed some food for us and packed up a parcel. She drove us to town, which was over an hour away. The first train arrived at eight she told us.

We waved her off and fell into each other's arms.

'God, that was scary,' I said.

'I can't believe she believed us.'

'I know,' I said, as we waited for the ticket office to open.

Finally, the train pulled in and we boarded it. Only then did we feel safe enough to relax.

'Thank God that's over,' Sheila said.

'I know. You see, these are the sort of stories people don't tell you about, the ones parents are always trying to scare you about. We're lucky nothing worse happened to us.'

'We should have twigged something wasn't right when we heard how much money they were paying,' I said.

'Yeah. I wonder if Anna knew?'

'Who knows. You know what Swedes are like? I hope we come across her again, though. I'd like to see the look on her face when we tell her.'

'Yeah, but don't forget she stayed the week. God knows what they all got into.'

'Hmm, wouldn't mind seeing footage of her. She had a great body remember?'

'Let's eat. I'm starving for lots of things now.'

Opening up the parcel of food we ate ravenously. When we'd finished off the fruit I saw a piece of paper at the bottom of the parcel. I pulled it out and opened it. There in neat handwriting were these words.

Check out, www.JillarooforaWeek on the web.
You're our first bona fide lesbians and I must say we certainly could tell the difference. No prompting needed.
You both look awesome.
Thanks for the footage.

Sheila and I just looked at each other, dumbfounded, and never said a word. After all what was there to say?

Illuminations
by Ruth Marie de la Flambeau

The narrow stairway descends sharply from the busy sidewalk. Taxis stir up rubbish and scattered leaves as we peer down into its depths. The doorway at the bottom looks small, so small we won't fit through it arm in arm. With a small squeeze of my hand, I untangle my arm from his and step down, keeping easy hold of his slender fingers behind me. He comes along willingly, if shyly.

Inside, the place is just as I'd imagined. Dimly lit. Simple. Tidy. Wooden tables with shining surfaces spaced evenly, almost all empty, save one or two in the back corner. The door closes quietly behind us, shutting out the autumn chill and the hustle of the Manhattan streets.

A pale waitress with seductive eyes and an innocent smile greets us and leads us to a table away from the others.

'Maggie,' she says, 'and Robert,' as she gestures to the table. 'Would you like to order a drink?'

'I think we need a minute,' I tell her.

'Of course.'

As her footfalls fade, I lift my eyes from the drinks menu to meet his. I gauge his intrigue and willingness to explore this new establishment for a moment, and then I raise an eyebrow. He does the same. I cock my head. He shrugs. I wait. He looks at me for a moment, and then lets a sly smile spread across his face. I nod and lift my hand to the waitress.

'Two martinis,' I tell her.

His eyes follow her slender form as she walks across the

room to the bar, and then shift back to me. I sit back, smooth my hair behind one ear and run one finger down its length, tracing it down across my sweater. His eyes follow, coming to rest on my nipple already beginning to harden against the lace of my bra.

He watches as my finger traces slow circles around it. He watches evenly, steadily, patiently. I love to tease him like this. The waitress brings our drinks and we sip them in silence, his eyes licking me patiently.

When she returns, she indicates I should follow her. I stand, turn, and glance back at him. He takes a sip of his drink and winks at me with sure confidence, so sure it belies a fluttering stomach beneath. I wink back and follow her through the door.

I am enveloped in complete blackness the moment I step through. Even sound doesn't penetrate the dark. I stand and wait. After a moment, hands take hold of my arms and walk me forward with sure knowledge of where we're going, though I can see nothing. I collide hard against a wall of softness – a thickly cushioned pillar by the feel of it, so wide my hands just meet on the other side where my wrists are tightly held together.

Hands unzip my skirt at the back and let it drop to my ankles, before peeling off the panties that had hidden beneath it. My shoes are removed and tossed away, leaving my stockinged feet standing damply on the cool floor. My hands are released briefly enough for my sweater and bra to be removed before my bare breasts are pressed back against the cushioning, wrists now tied together securely on the far side.

I seem to be left alone, though, for all I can tell, the owners of any numbered sets of hands could be just out of reach of my body. The only sense I have of the presence of anyone else is a slight breeze now and then, as of a body passing by. Otherwise, there is nothing; no sound, no vibration, nothing whatsoever to see.

148

After hugging the pole for quite some time, I jump, startled, as a pair of large hands wrap themselves around my ankles. And that's not all. As they hold firmly, two more snake up the back of my thighs and across my ass, grabbing and kneading at my bare skin.

What I have known as a pole pitches forward so that my arms and torso are lowered parallel to the floor, while my hips and legs remain standing. Bent over, with my ass now stuck out behind me, I feel the hands begin to explore its contours. The hands holding my ankles slide my legs apart to provide better access. I laugh out loud. The sound echoes around the room. I love that they are touching me, grabbing me, running their fingernails along my skin. I want them to claim me, hold me down, make me feel their touch.

As these first hands touch and arouse me, more hands appear, snaking up the insides of my thighs, smacking my ass, rubbing over the red marks no one can see in the blackness.

The physical sensation of being worked over by this many hands is one thing. That alone is worth the four months I waited to get a reservation for us here. What sets me moaning and makes my cunt begin to drip as they touch me, is my lack of control – knowing I have to take whatever they choose to do to me.

The hands soften, but keep touching. Feeling. Kneading. Teasing. Tantalising. And gradually, they push into my cunt. The invisible hands rub, tickle, slap and penetrate me until my cunt begs for more. She greedily takes in one, two, and then three fingers, wanting to be fucked wider and deeper.

The barrage of greedy hands is suddenly gone, leaving me panting. Sweat rolls across my forehead, as I lay draped across my perch. My wet thighs and arse feel the mysterious breezes with sharper clarity now.

Just as I silently begin to bemoan being left in a hungry state, my wrists are untied, my body is supported back to standing, and I am walked again through the darkness. I am pushed backwards to sit on what seems a bench or table, my feet set before me on a step of some kind, ropes secured around each of my stocking-covered thighs. Hands push me down onto my back without ceremony and tie my hands above my head.

The hands that have so deftly bound me in this new position now disappear, leaving me a moment to rest, to expand my senses once more into the darkness. I breathe slowly and collect myself, resting for the next experience.

A dim reddish light falls on something far away, over to the right of me. I can't tell for sure what it is, but it seems to be flesh. Just as quickly as it appeared, the light is gone. I wait. The darkness is complete again. Now light falls on something closer, close enough this time to see it clearly in the brief seconds it is illuminated: a cock, hard and thick, springing gently up and down as if it had just been freed of its shorts. The image stays burned on my eyes as the darkness returns.

The ropes around my thighs tighten. My legs are pulled a few inches apart. I struggle but the ropes are stronger than I am.

Reddish light flashes briefly on a scene to my left: Robert blindfolded and tied to an erect pole similar to the one I've known, save that he is tied with his back to it, his hands secured behind him around its girth. Our waitress kneels before him, rubbing her large breasts across the front of his trousers.

A light flashes to my right, the same hard cock, closer to me now, this time being stroked by a rugged practiced hand, drops of pre-come precariously close to dripping from its tip.

Darkness again. I force myself to breathe slowly; dizzy from the images I'm being fed. The ropes tighten and open me further.

On my left: her hand stroking his cock through his boxers, his head back against the pillar, his breath coming

150

faster. Darkness.

Again the cock on the right, this time so close I could touch it, were my hands not tightly bound above my head. The light stays on it for longer this time, giving me opportunity to appreciate the slickness of the shaft, the marbled veins, the wide glans just above the thick fingers still working it.

Cool air hits the innermost folds of my labia as the ropes pull my legs fully apart.

The woman is now on her knees, Robert's hard cock filling her mouth as her hands work his balls and stroke his thighs. He is no longer blindfolded, and looks down at her with fire in his eyes. The sight of her fucking his cock with her cherry lips makes me wet. I will the light to stay on them longer so I can keep watching, but a calloused hand grabs hold of my head and turns it as far as it will go to the right and holds it there. A cock pushes my lips apart, penetrating my mouth – the cock I was so recently seeing by the feel of it. I struggle to accommodate its girth as it pushes in and slides back out, deeper with each thrust until my throat is filled with it. My head is pressed down hard against the table as I take it deep, and then deeper until I can only gasp for breath each time it slides partway out.

Hands slide along my bound-open thighs and anchor on my hips. Something presses against the opening of my cunt, but I am too consumed by the rod being shoved down my throat to think much about it. My cunt gets hotter and wetter with each stroke across my tongue, she dilates further with each penetrating stretch of my throat. I smell rubber and I feel the other cock waiting until the one in my mouth has done its work. It waits as my arousal builds, waits as my gasps for air deepen, waits until my body arches and opens fully. Only then does it slide into my cunt on the new tide of arousal, slowly at first, and then all at once with the same force as the one in my mouth. Together the two cocks slam me, forcing their way into my body and then out of it again, if only for a brief second, each time leaving my body hungrier.

Redness burns through my eyelids and I know a light is shining on me lying here now, lying here being ravaged by two men at once, their cocks duelling to see who can penetrate my body more deeply. I hear Robert begin to moan and then yell out in his orgasm, as the woman's mouth sucking him and the sight of me being fucked overtake him. I feel his come slide down her throat at the same time as the one in my mouth spasms.

Out of nowhere, fingers are on my clit, rubbing in time with the shaft inside my cunt. My legs are somehow pulled further apart, my knees bent up to my belly, giving the cock deeper access. An orgasm begins to build in a dark low place in my body, rising to the surface with each stroke of the shaft, each brush of the fingers. I let my fucker tease it out of me, tease it up to the surface of awareness until it is all I can see, all I can taste, all I know. I let my body lie there and be righteously fucked until I too come screaming and writhing beneath this second man I will never see, who has just marked me as his own.

My eyes squint a little as I step back into the dimly lit outer room on shaky legs, smoothing my skirt down over my arse. I find Robert at the table where I left him, sipping his drink. I sit down carefully. He looks dishevelled, his hair tousled, his clothes wrinkled. Our eyes meet. We look at one another for a good long time. Then we finish our drinks.

All About the Sex
by Penelope Friday

It's all about the sex. It's all about his hands on me, ripping my clothing off me with bodily force, snarling in my ear that he wants me, that he wants me to beg, that he'll take me any and every way he fancies and I'll just beg him for more. It's all about that, because it's true. I want him to hurt me. I want to feel his fingernails digging into my flesh; his teeth gripping my shoulder like an animal. I want to feel his cock burning its way inside me so I'm aware of every single millimetre of him. I want him to pull my head back by the hair and bite my neck, vampire-like.

'Yes,' he says, kicking the door shut behind him, 'I know exactly what you want.'

I think I love him. Think, but am not sure, because I am drunk on the fucking, on my passionate need for him. And now, as I wait for him to touch me (he watches me with eyes that suggest that he knows exactly what I am thinking, exactly how desperate I am for him), I don't give a damn about love. This is about lust, pure heated lust, and I care for nothing but that.

'What are you doing here, Xavier?' I want to provoke him, and he knows it: knows that my words are chosen to fire up his angry passion. It is a game-which-is-not-a-game.

'There's only one thing I come here for.'

He leans back against the door, hands stuffed into his pockets. (And no, oh no, Xavier – I have other places for you to put those hands: many of them.)

'My stimulating ...' I leave a brief pause before adding, 'conversation, I take it?'

'Oh,' he drawls, his voice low and sensual, 'there are many other *stimulating* things about you, Carla.'

'I'm flattered.' I glance quickly at him, and look away.

'You should be more than flattered.' Xavier is giving me a long hot hungry look. 'What about it, Carla? Are your nipples rising up into sharp peaks of need? Is there a throbbing between your thighs as you think about what you want me to do to you – what I might choose to do?'

I shrug. 'I can live without you, Xavier,' I lie.

He gives a quick laugh. 'Without *me*, perhaps. But without this?'

He has moved towards me and pulled me into his arms. I can feel his erection, hard against my clit. This is one of the advantages of having a partner the same height as yourself: everything lines up just perfectly.

'Without what?' I breathe.

'Shall I go home?' he murmurs.

My hands, of their own accord, tighten around his back, even as I say, 'Yes.'

He presses his mouth against mine, opening his lips to allow his tongue to tease mine, while he runs his nails up my back.

'Shall I go home?' he asks again.

'No.'

It is the first submission. There will be more.

I hope.

He pushes his hand inside the waistband of my skirt. It cuts into my belly as his fingertips brush against my arse. 'You're sure about that? You want me to stay?'

'Maybe.'

The longer I draw out my defiance, the greater the sexual pleasure he (and I) will gain from my eventual compliance. We both know he can defeat me. We both want him to do so. But I will not make it easy for him. Why should I spoil our game?

'Oh, well.' He releases me, makes as if to go to the door. 'I'll see you around, yeah?'

'Xavier ...' I feel a sudden shot of fear. Once before, when I went too far, he left and did not return. He made me grovel before he agreed to come back.

'Carla?' he says, all innocent query, his hand reaching out to open the door.

I bite my lip. 'Please, Xavier, don't go.'

He grins. 'It's a "please" now, is it? That's a bit more like it.' His eyes meet mine meaningfully. 'Any more trouble from you, and I might just have to turn you over my knee and give that beautiful arse of yours a good paddling.'

I feel as if all the breath has been suddenly taken from my lungs. Xavier has never threatened (offered) corporal punishment before; I did not know before this second how much appeal the idea would have. His grin broadens.

'Why, Carla, I do believe you're turned on by that thought. What a kinky slut you turn out to be.'

'I'm not a slut,' I snap back at him.

He nods. 'You're right, Carla. Not *a* slut – *my* slut, isn't that right?'

'Prove it.' It is too much a plea. I had intended it to sound more a challenge.

'I will, Carla,' he promises, moving away from the door and dropping a light teasing, kiss on my lips. 'You know I will.'

God, I want him. So fucking much. If he asked me to lie down and grovel here and now for him, I'd do it. If he told me to follow him into the street and then fucked me there, I'd be willing. Sometimes the lust is nearer to hatred than love, and I even love that. I hate him for the fact that I'd do anything for him; I hate him for knowing it. And it's the hottest damn thing I know.

'Xavier ...'

'You're wet for me already.' He moves close to me, runs

155

a hand possessively down the side of my face, winding my hair through his fingers. 'I can smell your desire.'

He's a fine one to talk. I'm drugged by his scent; that pure testosterone mixed with the leather of his jacket. I could bury my face against him and breathe him in. He yanks on my hair, pulling my head back, exposing my neck.

'Bite me, oh please,' I think, only realising afterwards that I've said the words aloud.

He laughs, and runs the very tip of his tongue down my neck. 'There's a reason why people seem to have an obsession with vampirism, isn't there?' He raises his mouth to my ear and nibbles the lobe.

'Yes,' I say, scarcely knowing with what I am agreeing.

'Oh, babe, you want me,' he murmurs.

'Do not,' I hiss.

He sighs theatrically. 'I told you what would happen if I got any more trouble from you.' He lets go of me and looks around the room. 'Now, what have we got which might make a suitable paddle?'

'You wouldn't dare.'

'You think not?'

Xavier's eyes have lit on something over my left shoulder; I have to force myself not to turn to see what it is he is gazing at. Without his grasp on me, I can move. I tilt my head jauntily.

'I know you wouldn't.'

If anything will make him follow through, that will. He knows I'm intentionally baiting him – he's not an idiot – but I know that the idea turns him on as much as it does me. He'll take my bait. I hope.

'Want to bet?'

'Yes,' I say, trying to keep my arousal out of my voice. 'You haven't got the guts.'

Xavier's eyes seem to darken. 'You've asked for it, Carla,' he says, his molten chocolate voice having an edge of something fiercer. Chocolate with chilli, maybe – Xavier

156

is, after all, undeniably hot. He brushes past me, and pulls a book from my shelves. It is – perhaps appropriately – a hardback book on cocktails; long and thin. I have a different sort of cock in mind for tonight. It's long, but it's definitely not thin. 'On your knees and beg me for forgiveness, or across my lap getting what you deserve.'

Part of me wants to say, "Oh please, Xavier, both", but … I've begged before and I'll beg again. He's never spanked me, and oh God, I want him to. Plus, of course, I enjoy the role-play, pretending I don't want him.

'As if I'd get on my knees to you,' I defy him, ignoring all the occasions in the past when I have done just that.

'Take your knickers off and come over here.'

'And if I won't?'

'You will.'

He's right. I will. I slip my lacy knickers down my legs and walk over to him, my skirt rubbing against my arse as I hope Xavier's cock will – later. First, however …

'Now what?' I ask.

Xavier ensconces himself on the sofa. 'Now,' he drawls, 'you put yourself over my lap, face down.'

I can hear my heart beat so loudly in my ears I wonder if I'm about to faint. It seems I have enough left in me to obey Xavier's orders, however. When I'm lying across him, he pushes up my skirt so that it is ruched around my hips. I can feel his arousal; it pushes against my hip. I am desperate to slide down and slip his cock inside my mouth. I'm almost moaning aloud at the thought. Xavier puts one warm hand on my arse, and I wriggle closer in, putting more of my weight against his erection. Suddenly, however, the hand is removed and I feel a sharp swat as he slaps the book down against my buttocks.

I want him to do it again. God, I want him to do it again. It's as if I can feel every single nerve-ending in my arse, and they're all aflame. I want him to fan those flames.

'You're a very naughty little slut, Carla,' Xavier chastises

157

as he brings the book down again, this time focusing on my left buttock alone, quickly following it with a spank on my right. I'll be anything he wants as long as he goes on doing what he's doing.

'Yes,' I murmur.

He slaps the book against me several times in quick succession, building up a rhythm. I am humping his lap. Rubbing my clit against the inside of his thighs. I'm going to come any second, and he's not even touched me skin to skin.

'You deserve this, don't you?' he says, trying to keep his voice conversational. Even in the state I'm in, though, I know he's not as cool as he's trying to pretend. He's hard as a rock – but a damn sight sexier.

'Yes, yes, oh God, please.' There is a point at which pleasure becomes so intense that it's almost agonising. I am just – this – far from coming and he won't give me the satisfaction to bring me off. I'm almost crying. 'Please, Xavier. Please.'

I feel his cock twitch beneath me, and it's almost enough to send me over the edge. Fuck, Xavier, why have you never done this to me before? He slips a hand between us; unbuckles his belt, undoes his flies. His cock springs free: he's not wearing pants, but that's hardly a surprise.

'You're so fucking eager,' he says huskily, swatting me again and again, his cock pushing ever harder against me.

He slides one hand between my legs, his fingers warm against my clit. With his other hand clenched around the book, however, he still continues to punish me with heating blows against my arse. I can't take it any more, I can't. I can't. I don't fall over that cliff of orgasm so much as throw myself off and find myself flying. I'm screaming, I know, but it doesn't matter, it doesn't matter, I don't care.

Dimly, I'm aware of Xavier moving me, hitching my body off his legs, pushing me onto all fours before thrusting inside me; fucking me so insistently that I come again, almost before my first orgasm has finished. He's hard, and hot, and *fantastic* … and through the pounding of my heart I nevertheless hear him groan, feel him pulse inside me. He wants me as much as I want him, even though he'll never admit it. I need this. *We* need this.

When I come down, I'm back lying across Xavier's lap, gasping each breath. But before I have time to pull myself together, he's shrugged me aside, and, fastening his trousers, he strolls to the door, dropping a used condom into the bin, saying nothing more than, 'See you, Carla.'

Sometimes I hate him. It doesn't matter: it's all about the sex.

You're My Toy
by Sommer Marsden

It was the damnedest Christmas present I had ever seen. I pulled it out, held it up in all its blue silicone glory. 'What in the world?'

Aaron smiled and blushed. 'It's for you.'

'To wear?'

'No, it's for me to wear and for you to …'

'To?'

'Benefit from.' He laughed.

I could smell that new plastic smell, like lawn chairs or flip-flops, and I'd be a liar if I didn't admit that my pussy went wet when I looked at it. 'So when I get angry and call you a fuck-face you take me seriously?'

'Let me do it.' His hand crept up my thigh. All around us wrapping and ribbons and bows.

'Soon.' It made me nervous. I admit it. I wasn't sure why, but it almost seemed unfair to Aaron.

'Janie, Janie,' he sighed, climbing onto me, he pushed my thighs wide with his big knee and pushed his warm hands into my pyjama bottoms. His fingers slipped over my clit and then into me with such ease. I was so wet already. 'Don't you get it?'

'I think I'm about to,' I said, and then he kissed me quiet.

He tugged at my jammie bottoms, his mouth a wet trail from my lips to my belly button to my pussy. Hot perfect swirls of his tongue had me clutching the shiny silver wrapping and arching up to meet his mouth. 'I want to do it.

It's a present for me as much as for you. This way I'll be your toy.'

'I think I can deal with that.' I shut my eyes as he sucked my clit, pushing the flat of his tongue to my moist pussy. Aaron arched his rigid tongue into my cunt, fucking my pussy with his mouth only until I hauled him up by his hair, my shaking fingers twined in his dark locks. 'I will think it over while we …'

I spread my legs further, willing him to push his dick inside me, begging him with my movements to fuck me senseless.

'Bang like monkeys? Fuck like animals? Do the nasty?' Aaron laughed as he plunged into me, his hard cock tripping all the bundles of nerves deep inside me that made me pant like a dog while I came.

'Yes, yes, and yes!' I wrapped my legs around his flanks, pulling him into my pussy deeper so that the head of his cock pushed my g-spot.

Aaron decided to play dirty. He took a bright blue ribbon from the floor and tied me to the back of his mother's antique chair. Heavy dark wood carved with smiling moons and shooting stars. The thing weighed a ton and I was powerless to get at him. He pulled free of me as my body vibrated with urgency. I was right there on the crisp paper edge of coming and he was leaving me!

'Now listen, I don't want to rush you. And I don't want to push you.' He kissed my lips and I tasted my own juices on his mouth. He pushed his tongue deeper so that it was like sucking his cock. He nibbled my throat, my collar bone and my belly button before capturing a nipple in his mouth and sucking hard. The tug on my breast echoed in my cunt. A hollow sucking sensation that had me testing that damn ribbon and jerking the heavy wooden chair in a jittery dance.

'OK, fine, don't push me! Fuck me! It's Christmas! I need it,' I was at the point of begging and I simply didn't care.

'Let me do it then. Let me wear the strap on and fuck you until you cry,' he said, his mouth covering my vulva again, licking the sweet sticky juices of my need from my body. I tossed my hips at him like I was on a ship and begged.

'Please, oh fuck, please. Whatever you want.'

'Tomorrow? You'll let me do it tomorrow?'

'Yes, yes! Baby Jesus, merry Christmas, yes!' I shouted and pushed my pussy higher to him.

'Thanks, Rits. I love you baby. You're the best,' he laughed, kissing me so hard my scalp prickled from rug burn.

Aaron shoved his big hands under my ass cheeks, hoisting me a bit higher and angling me perfectly. When he shoved into me, balls deep and brisk, little purple and pink sparkles exploded in my vision. Five hard strokes, like he was driving nails or jack hammering concrete and I came, biting his shoulder so hard he growled. 'Don't make me bleed, Janie!' But he fucked me faster still, inching all three of us (me, him and the heavy antique chair) across the living room floor. When he finally came, we lay tangled and panting half under the Christmas tree. The chair had knocked off a few bulbs and a string of lights dangled like drunks after a long party.

'Tomorrow?'

He was all gentleness and butterfly kisses then. His fingers dancing over my skin so softly I shivered. I eyed the box and the somehow brutal-looking dildo erected from the face harness. Part of it scared the shit out of me and part of it made my cunt beat with an eager wet pulse. I nodded.

'Tomorrow,' I agreed.

All the next day I worried about it. Even when I answered the phone at work, in my head would be a big blue dildo on a black face mask. I could see Aaron coming at me, on hands and knees. A huge fake hard-on in front of him. I shook my head, trying to focus on what my customer was saying. But then my mind would switch it up. Me spread eagle against the basement wall, Aaron on his knees coming at me from behind. Fucking ms slow and sure and then fast and frantic with the bright plasticine dick.

'What?' I stammered. Three people hung up on me and my boss asked me if I'd had enough sleep.

I'd had plenty of sleep. I'd had sleep and sex all night long. Just the thought of using the toy on me had Aaron raring to go. Our whole evening had been spent in some form of debauchery or other. He had run me a strawberry scented bubbled bath and then run through our entire collection of toys. Rubbing my pussy and my tender clit with first the red marbled vibrator, then purple, then blue and then green. Who knew that we had such a rainbow's array of fake cocks in our house?

He had eaten my pussy until I babbled and then, giddy, exhausted and beyond coming again, I turned over and offered him my ass. Aaron had talked dirty the entire time. A fantasy-fuelled energized rabbit whose drum to bang happened to be, 'I'm going to fuck you so good, baby. I'm your toy. Say it, Janie. Say it, baby.'

'You're my toy,' I sighed, head down, body twisted in a pain pleasure combo as my loving husband spanked my ass and fucked me hard. He came, balls deep, holding onto my hips for dear life, coming into my back door.

Work was too much, I had to get home. I couldn't focus. My boss sent me out early. And there he was. Already home, already prepping. Flowers and candles and food galore. Fuck Face.

'I couldn't concentrate,' I confessed.

'Me neither.'

'I came home.'

'Me, too. Janie?'

He looked worried and my heart twisted a little. 'Yeah, baby?'

'You don't think it's too dirty, do you? It doesn't freak

164

you out, does it?'

I touched the evident bulge in his dust covered blue jeans. A mistake at work on a construction site could cost someone life or limb, I was glad he came home. 'No, Aaron. I think it's just dirty enough. So dirty, I could barely keep my head on straight. You've fucked me 60 different ways in that face harness today. In my head, but still …'

'And I want to do it for real. Now.' His hands were down in my pants, pushing into my cunt. Intrusive but in the best possible way. He invaded me with his big warm digits until I sank back against he counter, legs splayed like a fuck slut. My hands rubbed the length of his hard cock and I listened to him panting in a nearly desperate way. One of my favourite sounds in the world – out-of-his-mind-horny man.

'That would be good,' I laughed. He had my pants tangled down around my ass and my panties got caught. Aaron grabbed a paring knife from the counter and slit the sides –one, two easy as pie. He pushed the whole mess of clothing to the side and got on his knees. I watched him rub his hard pole through his pants and my eyelids sank down. I wanted him naked doing that.

'What?' His mouth pressed to me, his tongue wetting me perfectly. My clit, so swollen he could nibble on it, screamed for more.

'Take off your clothes. Do that naked. I like to watch you jack off.' I blushed when I said it, but I said it anyway. He was out of his clothes and digging under the tree as I unbuttoned my work blouse and unhooked my bra. I stood, shivering with goose bumps in the chilly kitchen.

When he came back, he held the face harness out to me and kneeled back down. His flushed hard-on poker straight from his slim hips, a glistening dot of pre-come rested on the swollen head. He sank himself face first into my pussy and resumed eating me out until I was absentmindedly rubbing the fake cock in my hands like a worry stone.

'Ready?' He smiled up at me. He had intended to get me

so horny and on edge that I couldn't give the face piece a second thought. And I didn't. I looked at it now and saw a big blue orgasm clutched in my hand.

'Ready.' I bent and strapped it on him. Aaron's hands trembled over the length of his dick, pumping so that he was close to purple and I knew from years of marriage, so close to coming a sneeze would set him off. 'Fuck me, Aaron.'

He sighed behind the mask and leaned in, shoving the appendage before him. My mind conjured up all things dirty and perverse: Unicorn horns; a Cyclops with a penis for an eye; riding a bike with a dildo seat. I shook my head. What was I thinking? But then I wasn't. He was shoving into me, his head going back and forth like he was giving a blow job. An inverted blow job. He was fucking me with his mouth and the cobalt blue dick that sprouted from between his lips.

I sprawled backwards on the counter, hips banging the grey granite workspace. Aaron stood, the protrusion on his face slippery with my juices. He pushed his hands under my ass, levering me up until I lay splayed on the cool surface, legs wide for him. He delved back in, hands encircling my ankles like flesh and blood cuffs. He fucked me hard, his head pistoning back and forth as I watched, mesmerized. I came, flooding his face and the leather tethers with wet sticky fluid. 'God, oh, God. Another. I want another.' Seeing him there, that way just for me was too much. I rolled to the side, pushing Aaron, 'Go, go, get on the counter.' I pushed at him. He arranged himself lengthwise on the counter like a patient on a hospital bed. My pussy quaked at seeing him that way, his permanent facial erection high and hard and waiting for me.

Aaron remained mute behind the fitted face piece. I couldn't see his mouth, but could tell from the laugh lines around his eyes that he was smiling. His hand pistoned along the length of his cock and I dropped down, sucking him into my mouth frantically. I swallowed his dick and inhaled deeply through my nose to let him into my throat.

All of him filled my throat and the rich smell of sex filled my nose. I cradled his balls in my hands, stroking him from dick to asshole until he mewled softly behind his mask. He fucked my mouth, his movements jittery, the reverse of what he'd just done to me. When he thrust too fast, I stilled him with my hand. 'No more. Wait.'

I crawled so that my pussy hovered over his face. I ran the smooth blue head of the cock over my dripping hole and locked eyes with Aaron. 'Do you want me to fuck your face, Aaron? Do you?'

Aaron nodded, his eyes sparkling with excitement and need. A muffled mmph passed for a yes.

I slid the head only into my wet pussy and locked my legs, my knees brushing the cool unforgiving stone. Aaron jerked his head up to thrust, his fist sliding up and down his rock hard dick. I levered up and away from him.

'Be a good boy or I won't let you. I'll leave you here hard and desperate and go back to work. Now that I've come I bet I can concentrate better.'

I was lying through my teeth, but he let his neck relax as he stroked his shaft and pleaded with his eyes.

I put the head back in, lowering inch by bright blue inch so that my thighs covered his ears and my cunt covered the phallus and Aaron's face. His hand flew over his erection, his hips thrusting up eagerly to the rhythm of his own sliding palm. I rode the face mask slow and sure. To make him suffer and to get him off. It was a win, win situation.

I gripped the edge of the counter, struggling to keep my composure and failing. I raised and lowered my hips, so fast, fucking myself with Aaron's extra cock that I thought I might smother him. I knew I hadn't when he reached up with a hand and gathered some of my juices on his finger. His other hand jacked his dick furiously, his knees coming up, feet pounding the counter. I pushed back and Aaron pushed his thick finger into my ass, slow and steady the way I like. He added a second as I slammed down over and over.

167

Finally coming in a rush of words and wetness.

I turned to see the thick spurts of pearly come sliding over his banged up knuckles, his dusty fingers, his perfect big fist.

I rested my head on the stone, trying to imagine what could be done with such a toy.

When I got the mask off of Aaron to kiss him, and kiss him I did, he solved the mystery.

'Tomorrow, meet me at Christine's after work.'

I got off at 3.00, he got off at 3.30. 'A bit early for dinner,' I muttered, licking the perfect sweet taste of my pussy off his lips.

'Not for dinner. Just for coffee. And for me.'

'You?'

'I'm going under the table.'

My knees were weak.

I actually thought I would pass out walking into Christine's. We'd been there a thousand times it seemed, but not with an agenda. The skirt that Aaron had picked out so carefully, swung and swished over my thigh high stockings. The hem kissed my tall black boots. As for panties, though, nothing but breeze. I was bare under the charcoal grey sheath skirt and my pussy begged for more attention from my man. I smiled to myself, fought the clawing anxiety over getting caught and walked into the dark restaurant.

The light was always set to ambient due to Christine's reputation as being the romantic eatery. The host found me and seated me at table three. 'The gentleman was here,' he said frowning. 'He must have excused himself for a moment. Can I get the lady a drink?'

Already a warm, heavy hand had curled around my stocking clad ankle. Another one was sliding up my inner calf with a whisper of nylon, a masculine unseen presence that left me trembling. I swallowed hard, smiled. 'I would love a nice big wine. Emphasis on the word big,' I joked.

The waiter frowned again but scampered off.

Aaron had pushed my skirt up above my knees so it puddled around my hips. I felt the smooth cool dildo slide along the slit of my pussy lips. I splayed my legs, biting the tip of my tongue to at least maintain a semblance of control. He nudged my opening with the tip of his tool and I slid a bit lower in my seat. My pulse slammed heavily in my ears and I was finding it hard to swallow even my own spit. Dizzy and horny and excited, I arched up to meet him just a bit and he slipped the cock home inside my moist hole.

'Oh, God.'

The server set my wine down and gave me a quizzical look. My fingers were twisted in the white linen table cloth and I could feel the twin spots of cherry red on my cheeks. 'Oh, God … that looks really, really good,' I managed.

He smiled, still looking wary of me. 'Yes, well, would you care to wait for the gentleman or can I get you …'

'I'll wait! I'll wait,' I sighed, because Aaron had slammed the bright blue dildo home. He pushed, craning the whole of his face forward to rub my g-spot with is new favourite toy. 'Jesus. I. Will. Wait.'

The host blinked and backed away from me. His eyes ping-ponged across the room for Aaron. God, I wondered what would happen if they found Aaron under there? That way. Big blue rod strapped to his face, fucking his wife under the table like a whore? What would happen?

I'll tell you what did happen. I came at the thought. I came, biting my tongue, clenching my jaw and my wine glass. I waited for the delicate crystal stem to shatter, but it didn't. I waited for Aaron to stop, but he didn't.

He kept fucking me.

I took a swig of wine and our actual waiter appeared. 'Hi, I'm Ed and I'll be your … are you OK?'

Aaron had my thighs pinned wide in the ladder back chair. One of my hands gripped my butter knife, no clue why, and the other the edge of the seat for balance. He had

169

the long fake dick buried deep in my pussy by then and he was swirling it. Great looping motions that managed to trip every good nerve I possessed. His fingers pressed and stroked over my clit and I held my breath until spots appeared in my vision. Fingers on my swollen button, fingers probing my ass, and his face swishing and whirling that blue monstrosity deep into the wet well of my cunt.

'I am fine!' I crowed as I came, a long unwinding orgasm that for some reason set me to laughing. Maybe it was the venue. Maybe it was the release.

I heard the slapping frantic sounds of my wonderful, polite, upstanding husband beating off under the table like a common john and a blip of pleasure rolled through my pelvis. A little amused bouche of an orgasm. I heard a muffled grunt and sigh as hot, sticky come splashed on my thighs and knees. He was painting me.

This waiter was adorable. I saw his eyes take in just the heel of Aaron's boot. He was on to us. I heard the jingle jangle of the harness's rings and felt it drop at my feet.

'If the lady and gentlemen would like some more time, I can come back.' He had backed up three steps, our waiter. Back far enough for me to see the exquisite hard-on tenting his plain black server pants. I ran my tongue over my bottom lip.

There was another fantasy that Aaron and I had discussed … a third party.

'No. I think we're good,' Aaron said, plopping into his chair. His hair stood up in whirls and horns and his face was flushed and slightly damp by his lips. That was me on his face. I shivered.

'Very well. Can I get you an appetizer?'

'Another one?' Aaron joked.

I laughed. Our waiter crept closer, sharing our secret, somehow drawn by it. He leaned in close, order pad in hand. 'I'm sure very little could top that one,' he said, eyes darting to me and then my husband.

Aaron grinned. His hand found my thigh under the table where my skirt still rode high around my hips. I knew he was thinking what I was thinking. 'So, Ed, would you be offended if someone called you fuck face?' my man whispered. 'And how are you at the whole sharing thing? Are you a good sharer, Ed?'

Ed was smiling but I was more focused on the bulge in his trousers and the mental image I had of him sporting a big blue cock from his pretty boy face.

I liked my new toy. I liked it a lot.

The Devil's Harlot
by Morgan Honeyman

Having placed the ad in the Personals, Sophie tried not to wait around for the phone to ring. She kept herself busy with ironing and reading so she didn't just sit staring at the phone. Then, next day at work, her thoughts wandered to what kind of man would answer and more importantly, would she have enough courage to go through with the deed?

The first call came five minutes after she had arrived home from work. She hesitated as the rings echoed through the room. Her mouth grew dry and the butterflies in her stomach woke up. Sophie listened to the voice. It was a nice voice. It wasn't the voice she wanted. She didn't quite know why it wasn't right but she did know that when she heard the right voice, that it would be the man for her.

Ten phone calls later, Sophie was beginning to think she had made a big mistake. All the men sounded nice, extremely willing, and totally unsuitable. Sighing, Sophie poured herself a large glass of crisp cold wine, kicked off her shoes and flicked on the television. The phone rang again. Sophie glanced at the clock. The call was late and she considered ignoring it.

Smiling to herself, Sophie put down the phone. It was the call she had been waiting for. If anyone had asked her what made this call stand out from the others, she couldn't have said.

There had been a couple more phone calls between her

and the man, but no exchange of photographs. It seemed the best course of action, but it was a gamble for both of them.

Now, Sophie sat nervously at the bar. Sipping her drink, she turned and watched the people going about their business. It was a trendy wine bar, one she wouldn't normally frequent, all shiny chrome and brown suede, overcrowded with super egos and dull business talk. A young man behind the bar gave her a cheeky smile. She returned it with an added wink. Sophie knew she looked good and tonight she wanted to play a different role from her usual impression of a wallflower. Her clothing gave nothing away of the game she was about to play. She was deliberately dressed in a conservative skirt and blouse. The look she was aiming for was pure Sunday-school teacher. Only her shiny stiletto shoes looked slightly risqué. Crossing her black stocking-clad legs, she looked towards the door, trying to guess which man was the one who had rung all the bells.

She was busy watching a couple in a booth, doing everything but make love, when a voice made her jump.

'Sophie?'

She turned and stared, momentarily confused.

'I'm Jack.'

He held out his hand and Sophie shook it. The grip was firm, steady and, more importantly, dry. Sophie hated a clammy handshake and was pleased that the man didn't disappoint. As she ordered another drink for Jack and herself, Sophie looked over the young man standing next to her. He was, at a guess, 20 years younger than her, which was exactly what she had asked for. That he hadn't turned and run away was another major plus point. Sophie had been unsure how many young men would want to fulfil a middle-aged woman's fantasy. Surprisingly, there had been quite a few.

The advert hadn't said good-looking, but Jack had a ruggedness that was appealing. She'd never been overly

174

keen on the chocolate-box, square-jawed, hero look. He also had a hint of bewildered innocence, which was an even bigger turn-on. As she took a sip of wine, she looked around and wondered what the surrounding people made of them. Did they think she was his mother? His boss? What would they think if they knew she was already moist with arousal? Her hardened nipples rasped against the lace on her bra. Sophie uncrossed and then re-crossed her legs, squeezing her thighs tight to increase the intensity of the tension.

'I think it's about time we got out of here.' She drank the last of the wine and looked directly into Jack's eyes. He nodded.

In the taxi back to her apartment, they didn't speak much. Exchanging information, talking mundane pleasantries would spoil the mood. Sophie didn't want to see the real man behind the fantasy and, she was damn sure, Jack didn't want to know the ins and outs of the life of a middle-aged woman either. By the time they got to her front door, the doubts and insanity of the situation were beginning to make her anxious. Sophie fumbled with the key. His gentle hand covering her own steadied her nerves.

They stood in the middle of the living room, Jack looking around at the décor, or for a way to escape. Sophie wasn't sure which.

'The outfit is in the bedroom. Through there.' Sophie pointed to the spare room, the garment and accessories laid out in readiness. She turned towards the mirror, reaching out towards the mantelpiece for the lipstick that had been deliberately left out ready for this moment. Lining her lips in scarlet, Sophie undid the pins in her hair, letting it hang loosely around her shoulders. Undoing the top two buttons on her blouse, the look was complete. The door opened behind her and she turned.

The dampness between her thighs increased, along with the rush of arousal deep within her. Sophie looked over Jack, his black outfit standing out in the colourful room. She slowly moved forward, her hands shaking. As they approached each other, their eyes met and the understanding that everything would be all right passed between them.

Sophie fell to her knees and clasped Jack's legs. 'Forgive me, Father, for I have sinned.'

She buried her face deep into the fabric of the cassock, pressing her cheek against the telltale bulge of Jack's hardening cock.

Jack rested his hand on her head. 'Bless you, my child. I will help you with God's forgiveness.'

Sophie looked up at Jack, the white collar stark against the black fabric, and for a moment the plain, gold cross around his neck held her gaze. She kissed the cloth-covered erection in thanks and stood.

'What do you want me to do, Father?'

'I have to drive the evil of the devil out of you and replace it with my goodness.'

Sophie bowed her head. 'How will you do that, Father?'

'Go and lie down on the bed, my child, and I will show you the way to forgiveness.'

Stretching out on the silk sheets, Sophie waited in silence for Father Jack to walk into the room. Seconds passed and when he finally entered, Jack stood at the side of the bed, looking down at Sophie. He reached over, holding eye contact all the time. Grabbing the edges of the silk blouse, he ripped it open, the buttons flying in a myriad of directions.

'You dress like the devil's harlot. Take off those garments of shame.'

Sophie slipped down the skirt and pulled off the blouse, throwing them to the floor. She was pleased to hear Jack moan as he looked over her body, dressed in a red and black lace basque and silk stockings encasing the long legs. He lay beside her, holding her face gently before kissing hard and thrusting in his tongue. When he'd had his fill of the hungry mouth, Jack pulled away.

'Shame on you, you strumpet of Satan. I try to wipe off the sluttish lip colour and you suck on my tongue, trying to tempt me, a servant of God, into sin. You are beyond redemption.'

'Father, forgive me.' Sophie found it hard to breathe as the fire of need consumed her body. 'I know not what I do. I burn with the fire of lust. I need salvation.'

'Undo the laces on your garment. Free your breasts so I can inspect them for signs of your sins.'

Sophie's shaking hands undid the ties. Jack smiled and cupped a full, creamy mound, rubbing his thumb lightly across the rosy bud.

'Don't be afraid, my child. First I need to test you, then I need to cleanse you of your sins.'

Sophie arched up into his touch as Jack slowly sucked and toyed with her hardening nipple. By the time he moved on to her other breast, Sophie was desperate for Jack's hand between her legs. She groaned in pleasure and frustration as he continued to lick, suck and kiss her breasts. When she though she couldn't stand it any longer, Jack's hand touched her through the material of her panties.

'You are wet with the devil's juices.' He sat up on the side of the bed. 'I can see you are more possessed than I thought. Drape yourself over my legs and prepare to have the Devil's lust beaten out of you.'

For a moment, Sophie hesitated. Spanking, or whatever he had in mind, had not been in the instructions she had emailed him. The uncertainty only lasted a few seconds. Before positioning herself across his knees, she glanced at the bulge in his cassock. It held much promise and she licked her lips at the thought.

'Ouch,' she yelped at the first gentle stroke.

'Did you enjoy that?'

'Yes, Father,' she answered truthfully.

'Then the Devil is still in you.'

The next slap was a little harder. As she gave out a

mixture of a yelp and a moan, Sophie spread her legs a little hoping that Jack would pick up the hint that she wanted more.

'Are you trying to tempt me off the righteous path?'

'No, Father. The Devil is making me squirm with sinful desire. I am just trying to relieve the awful need between my legs.'

'Let me test you.' Tantalising slowly, he pulled down her panties. His hand stroked her tingling arse cheeks before he gave her a hard spank on her bare skin.

Sophie relished the arousal that was building up in her, wanting desperately for him to touch her and at the same time, wanting to put off the moment. His hand slid down, cupping her cheeks before finding her neglected and soaking pussy. His finger slipped in without any resistance. He groaned and the game was forgotten for a moment as he frigged her until the juices ran down her leg. As the blunt fingers gave her the touch she needed, her clit rubbed against the rough material of the cassock.

'Oh, God.' She screamed as her climax began to build inside her.

'That's it, child, you call out for God's forgiveness.'

'Please more. More. Oh, God, more.' As the feelings inside were ready to explode, Jack withdrew his fingers and brought his hand down hard on her backside. She screamed out, her whole body trembling at the force of her orgasm.

'Oh, that was ...'

'Quiet. We have driven the devil out but now I will have to cleanse you before you will be ready to accept the goodness that is between my legs.' He picked her up and threw her on the bed. Roughly, he pulled off her silk panties. As Jack opened her legs for more access she closed her, eyes wanting to block out any sensation except the ones Jack was giving her. She cried out at the first touch of his tongue. He suckled, he licked and he nipped. Jack touched the core of her being. Sophie shook, as wave after wave of pleasure filled her body. Stretching out in pure satisfaction, Sophie was vaguely aware that Jack was slipping on a condom.

'Now, you harlot of the Devil, I am going to take away the badness in your body and replace it with my goodness.'

Instead of thrusting in, Jack lay on top of her, kissing her neck before giving her a lingering kiss on the lips. As she concentrated on the tongue that was teasing her ear and causing her whole body to shiver, she didn't feel the tip of his cock penetrate her. A second later, Sophie bit her lip as she was filled with a hardness and fullness she hadn't felt in a long time. Her legs wrapped around Jack's waist, the material of the cassock rubbing against her thighs, adding to the sensations.

'Feel me filling you, taking you, possessing you,' Jack whispered in Sophie's ear. 'You are mine.'

'Yes, Father.' Sophie threw her head back as her body jerked to a second climax. 'I am your faithful servant.'

'You are a dirty whore who has to suffer for her sins. This will not be quick or easy.' Jack moaned and pushed in hard.

'I am prepared to take everything you …' She arched her body. 'Want …' Her legs clasped hard around his waist. 'To give me.'

Jack stopped moving, pulled out and moved off the bed. For a moment, Sophie felt afraid that he'd had a change of heart though his hard cock told her a different story.

'Your lust is burning me with its fire,' he said, before pulling off the cassock.

She looked over his naked body with admiration. The well developed shoulders, broad chest and flat stomach showed a devotion to the gym. Her eyes travelled up the muscular thighs, glistening erection, all the way up to hold his gaze.

'Are you coveting my body, you harlot?'

'I'm sorry, Father, I'm overcome with shameful thoughts about your holy person. Forgive me.'

He climbed back on the bed, grabbing her wrists and pulling her arms up above her head, pinning her down. Their sweaty, hot bodies glided against each other as he pierced her with his holy shaft. There was no more talking he thrust in and out and she arched her body for more contact. One last push and his body shook as his orgasm overtook him. He slid off her, breathing heavily at her side. In the intense atmosphere of the room, the only noise that could be heard was their heavy breathing and the tick tock of the old fashioned clock on her bedside table.

The spell was broken. The pretence ended. As he sat on the edge of the bed, Sophie looked at the broad back and wanted desperately to ask him to stay, but knew that wasn't part of the deal. 'The shower is through there, second door on the right.'

There was no mention in the advert about staying or making love like a man and a woman, as themselves. He got up without looking at her and walked out of the room. For a moment, she lay in bed looking up at the ceiling and deciding whether she had more balls than to hide in the bedroom. Climbing out of bed, Sophie stood and wrapped a silk robe around her body, walking into the kitchen to put the kettle on. She sensed rather than heard him come up behind her. She turned. Jack took a step towards Sophie and kissed her lightly on the lips.

'That was amazing. If you ever want to repeat this experience, let me know.'

Sophie took a deep breath, feeling his eyes lingering on her body. 'I will.'

Jack's hand rested on the door handle, for a moment he seemed reluctant to leave.

'Or if you've any fantasies of your own.' Sophie called out to his retreating back.

Jack turned. 'It's funny you should mention that. I have a sheriff's badge at home. I always fancied myself as a cowboy.'

Sophie leant against the wall and hoped the look on her face was one of seduction and not one of complete insanity. 'And what part would I play?'

Jack looked her up and down. 'You'd be the pretty Indian squaw.'

'And what would happen between the hunky cowboy and the innocent squaw?'

He tipped his head to one side. 'She'd be bathing and the cowboy would come up behind her, drag her to his camp, throw her roughly to the floor, tie her up and torture her with his tongue and his hands until she told him all he wanted to know. Then he would take her back to his log cabin and have his wicked way with her, again and again.'

Sophie gritted her teeth against the new wave of arousal that was threatening to take away any semblance of rational thought. She could see the outline of his cock, which was hardening again. The warmth between her legs told her, what she already knew – that the idea appealed. She fought against asking him to stay.

'Same time, next week?' Her hand rubbed her left breast as she smiled at him.

'I'll look forward to it.' Jack answered, as he held her gaze, his hand rubbing the outline of his growing bulge.

Sophie sighed contentedly as the door closed behind her fantasy lover. Now she just needed to find a squaw outfit and some soft rope.

Hugs, Kisses, Dominatrices
by Tara S Nichols

There was no way getting around it, my new roommate was a piece of work. Sure, she was deceivingly pretty, with a small ski-jump nose and perfect pouting lips, but her stiff, dyed black hair could moonlight as a spare bottle opener if we ever found ourselves one short. Her hard blue eyes blazed with an intimidating intelligence, but her temperament was as prickly as the studs on the leather collar she wore around her neck.

She looked at me with disdain, as though she already knew everything about me, neatly slotting me under some despicably boring category with other mousey men. She wasn't too far off, to be honest, but I have to say I wasn't too impressed with her, either.

I felt tricked. With a name like Elliot, I never would have guessed she was a she, let alone a hard core Goth girl. Had I the wherewithal to challenge her, I would have evicted her the moment I laid eyes on her, rather than gawk across the apartment at her.

It had only been two weeks since she'd moved in, but already I was being crowded out. I don't mind a little eccentricity, a piercing here and there, or an extra couple of guests in the abode, but our small, shared apartment looked like a black and blue ball, and I was its resident wallflower.

Every night chaos went on, and every day she ate my food, used my bath towel, shoved my furniture against the wall to make room for her yoga mats, and insisted on a black light in the bathroom. (Brushing my teeth would never be the same again.)

She had no idea what a coaster was, so my nice polished antique furniture looked as though it had been attacked by an amorous octopus. After two days I developed hyper tension, after the third, my right arm went numb. Out of fear for my personal belongings, I started to hoard them in my own room.

Night after night I watched as the other half moshed on my polished hardwood floors, scuffing and scratching my damage deposit away. Then, after everyone had gone home, I'd hear strange whirring sounds of unidentifiable electronics coming from her bedroom, and her telltale sighs as she pleasured her way 'til dawn. Despite her efforts, she emerged every morning just as surly as when she went in.

All I really wanted was someone whom I could relate to, perhaps watch a few movies with, or even play a round of cards, but that was not to be the case. Ours was a relationship based on wariness and sleeplessness.

My lack of sleep had weathered my patience and brought me to a dangerous level I thought beyond me, that is, until I dared to make a snide comment about her investing in the battery stock market. She took my hostility in stride, perhaps feeding upon it as though it nourished her, and flashed me a sweet, knowing smile before she left the apartment for the day.

It was in that smile where I realised my feelings had morphed, jumped ship, or mutated, for my heart did a back flip and my palms grew slick with sweat. How she'd managed to penetrate my defences, to worry her way through my values and my morals, and nestle deep in my heart, I don't know, but there she was. Soon all I could think about was how to replace that vibrating machine she kept hidden behind her bedroom door with myself.

I'm not a womaniser, a charlatan, or a gigolo by any stretch of the imagination, but at that moment something inside me snapped, and the next thing I knew I had a hard-on that could pogo vault the high bar, and pants too loose to hide it.

She was so damn bad it was intoxicating. Just her presence gave me such a stiff erection I feared I might go blind from an imbalance of blood flowing through my body. When she wore outfits like the short black flared skirt that barely covered her ass, with black and white striped leggings nipping at the bottom of her garter belt, it was a miracle I didn't rupture a seam in my finely ironed slacks. Then again, even her waitress uniform, a peach and white T-shirt dress fashioned from the 1950s, left me at full salute for at least an hour after she left for her shift.

I wanted to bury my face in her push-up bra cleavage and set up residence in her underwear. I wanted her to pull that loose thread that held me so rigid and keep pulling until I completely unravelled. I had it bad, so bad I was delusional.

But now, with her gone for the day, I could finally have the place to myself. I could try to reclaim my identity, my wits, and maybe even my apartment for a few hours.

I flipped the stereo on and readjusted the dial to my preferred station. I retrieved my hidden stash of wholesome cereal from the top shelf in the kitchen, and settled into my easy chair intending to read a novel.

Strangely enough, I couldn't concentrate. I set the book down, letting my gaze settle on her bedroom door. It was no use. Her mysterious presence still gripped me even in her absence. My curiosity about her and what went on in her bedroom gnawed at me until it had successfully distracted me from the safe doldrums of my own life.

I suspected she knew I longed to peek inside, had become aware of my keen interest in the contents of her highly guarded abode. If I didn't know better, she was trying to make me curious, only opening the door a crack and slipping through the narrowest possible gap, wrapping herself in little more than a face cloth, then scampering dripping wet, fresh from the shower, to her bedroom, knowing full well I was sitting in the living room.

There were other incidences as well, but the thought that she might be interested in a guy like me seemed utterly ridiculous.

Until she came along, I was comfortable with the way I presented myself to the world, but now I questioned my upper class wardrobe, my wall of well-read literature, and the fact that I managed to save at least half my pay cheque. So I didn't go out every Friday night, or any night, for that matter, and maybe I could use a little airing out, but for as much fault as I could find in myself, I could see the equal amount, if not double, in her lifestyle.

No, she'd never find me attractive.

That settled, I flipped my newspaper open, snapping the spine taut, and prepared to enjoy my evening of solitude.

One minute later my mind returned to the bedroom door.

Lowering the newspaper, I peered across the room to the wooden barricade and thought, perhaps, it was ajar.

Standing up, I stared at it. Yes, it was ajar. I hurried over to the window and drew the drapes. She'd never know if I took a peek, stole inside for merely a glimpse of her mysterious den. As long as I maintained the boundary, her room and everything that she kept from me would haunt me. The only way to get over her was to break the spell.

I ventured closer for a look. The room was dark and I knew I'd have to stick my arm in so I could turn on the light, and in doing so, widen the gap. I gave the knob a cautious little push sending the door swinging inward, and then quickly stepped back. I half expected to find it booby trapped, but to my surprise, nothing happened.

I took two measured breaths, giving my heart a moment to slow down. Then, pawing the wall, I found the light switch and flipped it on.

A moment later I wished for the darkness once again. My mouth dropped open at the sight that greeted me. Walls painted a high gloss black gleamed so bright I had to shade my eyes. A squat dresser wrapped in black vinyl and fastened with enough metal studs to outfit an army of punks lurked like an overgrown spider along the wall opposite where I stood, the handles like nose rings, the ornate curve of the leg making it seem ready to pounce. Instruments of pleasure spread across the dress top; latex and rubber coated devices meticulously laid out, much as one would find at a surgeon's table. A matching trunk with the lid ajar clamped down on red satiny fabrics that looked as though their attempt to escape had failed. A taller dresser, littered with make-up, perfumes, and jewellery, stood in the corner closest to me, a rainbow of frilly underwear hanging out of the top drawer along with a pair of silver handcuffs.

Then there was the apparatus hovering over Elliot's bed, a contraption made up of harnesses suspended from the ceiling. Thick, sturdy bolts had been driven through the plasterwork and anchored into the joists, a task I felt certain had been done on a day I'd been out. Rings of some tensile strength steel looped through the bolts, and those in turn held a web of ropes and restraints up off the ground. Nestled among the straps, the ropes, and the restraints was a leather seat with a shiny black dildo mounted in the centre. I spun on one heel taking in each clashing object as though under physical assault.

I'd never seen such a misuse of hardware in my life, but most appalling of all was how my body responded to the endless possibilities the contraption and dresser top gadgets inspired. My cock stirred, stiffened, and filled until it nudged the button holding my pants closed at the waist. My sac tightened as I envisioned the spectacular event of my naked form strapped into that harness and my freewill taken away.

How could I want such a thing?

I shifted with unease, feeling betrayed by my own body, and told myself it was time to go. Unfortunately, my feet stayed their ground and my eyes mutinied, my gaze wandering beneath the contraption to the downy soft contours of Elliot's bed located just below.

Her bed seemed so innocent in contrast to the rest of the room. Rumpled and soothing, her red flannel sheets revealed a softer side to the impatient, scowling roommate I'd come to know. I couldn't help but smile at the sight of a pair of flannel pyjamas that lay discarded on the floor. I reached for them, but stopped when something caught my eye. Something long, pink, and out of place had become tangled up in her sheets.

Uncovering the item, my eyes widened at the sight of what had to be the most intimidating dildo ever made. It wasn't so much the size of the mechanism, as the shape of it. Picking it up, I inspected the gnarled surface with awe, pushed against the cushiony silicone to find it resilient yet formidable, and overall, was impressed with the handiwork that went into making the darn thing.

It was then I noticed the small black button on the base of the handle, and I beamed, feeling certain I'd just uncovered the source of the mysterious late night whirring noise. I turned it on with a simple flick.

Unprepared for the sheer power the device commanded, my wrist began to vibrate. My fingers gripped the cylindrical object tighter, but the mechanical devil was determined to break loose. For a moment all I could do was stare at the blur my arm had become. Then, grabbing hold of the tip with my other hand, I hung on in a vain attempt to wrestle it to the off switch. The dildo proved to be a cunning opponent, shaking me to the point where my teeth rattled and I'd lost all feeling in my left arm. Before I could stop it, the device broke free of my grasp and went sailing across the room. It crashed against the far wall with a sickening crunch.

I raced to the scene and scooped it up, but it flopped over like a drunkard. A whimper escaped my lips and I shook it to hear the shards tinkling inside. My guts constricted at the sound.

Not good. Not good. I panicked.

Glue! Glue! Glue! was all I could think. Where in tarnation did I keep the glue?

Had I been calmer I would have noticed the snick of the key in the lock, would have become alarmed at the sound of Elliot's footsteps pounding across the living room, but in my distress, I did not.

Elliot reached the door. 'What the hell do you think you are doing?' she demanded, her fury always ready at the surface. I looked up to see the firm line of her mouth and noted how beautiful she looked when she was angry.

Then her eyes fell to what I held in my hand, the pink rubbery phallus flaccid against my wrist.

Finally my disillusionment that I could repair the damage left me and fear settled in. 'I didn't mean to – it just …' I floundered, knowing full well I was a dead man.

'My dildo! My favourite dildo!' She streamlined over to where I stood and snatched the broken sex toy from my cold sweaty fingers.

'I'll buy you a new one,' I said, trying to take it back, trying to read the model number.

'You can't! This one was custom made.'

Some strange perversion in me wanted to ask how one got fitted for such a gadget, but thankfully self preservation kicked in and I pressed my lips tightly together.

'I came home early just for this.' She shook it in front of my face. 'You can't imagine how shitty my day has been, how crappy my day job is. All I was looking forward to was a little one-on-one with Goliath here, and now, I can't even have that!' She pierced me with a determined stare. I felt like a mouse about to be devoured.

'Listen,' I scrambled backward until my shoulders bumped against the bed. 'We can get to the bottom of this like reasonable adults.'

'Oh yes, I couldn't agree more. This is very much an adult situation.' She stalked toward me, closing the distance with the speed of a cheetah. She lowered down on to her haunches to look me in the eye, but all I could concentrate on was the fact that I could see up her skirt where her garter fastened to her sheer hot pink nylons.

'This is a very serious predicament you've put yourself in, one I somewhat suspect you did on purpose.' She continued in her intimidating tone, snapping my attention away from her thigh. 'You've disrupted the sanctity of my private space.'

At the mention of her bedroom I couldn't help take the opportunity to comment on her décor.

'About that ...' I pointed meekly to the wall. 'You owe me a damage deposit. Perhaps we could call it even?'

Her eyes widened and her scowl deepened. 'Even?' she seethed. 'What you need is to be punished. If you were one of my subjects I'd be most severe with you.'

'Punished? Subjects?' I sputtered. 'What are you, the headmistress of some satanic cult?'

She threw her head back and laughed. 'No, sugar. Nothing so glamorous.' She brought one pointed fingernail under my chin and applied enough pressure as to make me raise my face higher. 'I'm a dom.'

'A dom? You mean ...' I motioned toward the device.

'A dominatrix, yes. I strap lovers in there, and they beg me to give me a hard time.' Her gaze lingered on the dildo on the seat and a sly smile tugged at her mouth as though she remembered something fondly. 'The harness is for them, but that ...' she pointed to the broken phallus, 'was just for me.'

I swallowed hard, driving the point of her nail into my skin in the process. If I was a mouse, then she was definitely the cat in this analogy, a real sexy pussy about to swallow me whole. For some reason the thought turned me on.

'The way I look at it, Mister, is you owe me a good time.'

'I what?' I edged back flabbergasted.

'Come on, it's not like you haven't been thinking about it. I've seen the way you watch me. I know you sniff my shampoo and swipe the odd pair of panties out of the laundry.'

'I don't. I …'

'It's all right. In fact, I think it's kind of cute. I'll even admit to tormenting you a bit just to see what it took to make you snap, but you've got great resolve.'

Upon hearing that, I sat up in a hurry. 'I knew it!'

One of her manicured eyebrows rose and I settled back into the place where I'd been cowering.

Her face hovered closer to mine, but now I could see the mischief dancing in her eyes. 'You've got a warrior tucked away in that geeky little heart of yours, don't you?'

'I'm not a geek, I just dress well.'

'Trust me, you'd look better in leather assless chaps.'

'That's not going to happen, and come to think of it, this has gone on long enough.' I made to stand up but she placed her palm against my chest. I remained where I was, as though I truly believed she could physically stop me.

To my surprise she leaned back on her heels, her hands going to the tiny buttons lining the front of her uniform. I watched dumbstruck as she nimbly pried each button free, shrinking the gap between me and her hot pink satin bra beneath.

My heart pounded against my rib cage and I tugged at my collar.

She chuckled at my actions. 'Don't worry, string bean, I'm not going to make you do anything you don't want to.'

With the last buttons free, she peeled the short T-shirt dress off her shoulders and shook it away from her arms. Her breasts bounced with her efforts and I stifled a groan as my cock twitched and tried to lurch off my body and into hers.

'That's so much better,' she said with an overly dramatic

sigh. 'Now ... how do you like it?' She tapped one finger against her bottom lip. 'Plain? Safe? Traditional?' She leaned forward so her cleavage lay inches from my mouth. I salivated as though she were a rare delicacy, a buffet upon which I was about to gorge. 'Are you a man who likes it from behind, standing up, or with a woman on top?' She leaned back again, and speared me with a sly smile. 'No, not missionary for you. I've seen you sneak a few barbeque chips from the table, and I know you have a hidden stash of extra hot sauce in your cupboard.'

I felt her fingertip under my chin again, and merciless in her pursuit, she forced me to look her in the eye. 'You like a little fire, don't you? You like powerful women rather than meek little kittens.' She reached out and gripped my shoulders, encouraging me to stand. Like a puppet I obeyed.

Her fingers went to work on the fasteners of my pants and in no time she'd dropped them along with my underwear to the floor. I stood before her, shamefaced and erect. Everything she had accused me of had been true. I liked her rough treatment of me, the dirty talk, powerful women. I believed my cock capable of doing back flips if she commanded it. At that point the worst thing she could do to punish me was send me on my way, tell me to amble off to my own room and never bother her again.

'I'm impressed,' she said, and I breathed a sigh of relief.

With a sudden shove of her hands, she sent me toppling onto the bed. Crawling on top of me, she gripped the sides of my shirt and with a mighty heave, tore my top open. Buttons flew everywhere.

I started to protest but fell silent when her bra came off. Round tits, as big as grapefruits, tumbled free, and my mouth fell open as she cupped and squeezed them together. Dark red nipples that pointed to the ceiling beckoned to me and I raised my hands to touch, but she slapped them away with a laugh.

Leaning her naked breasts against me, she slid the shirt

over my shoulders, and I unwittingly found myself trapped. The next moment I felt her tongue, hot and wet, tracing circles around my nipple. I moaned as she sucked, bit, and licked each one to a tiny point. I arched my hips, loving every minute of it. It was almost too good to believe.

'This isn't real,' I gasped.

'It sure is, and it feels damn nice.' She jerked her hips to punctuate her point. 'Look down, look where your cock is.'

As I craned my neck to look, she pulled the strings on both sides of her panties and the fabric fell like feathers, exposing her shapely hips and a hint of hair gracing her mound. Most impressive though, was the fact that the shaft of my cock had burrowed a tunnel between her pussy lips and lay snug against her clit as she rocked back and forth. My breath caught in my throat.

She smiled. 'Give yourself a break. You're the kind of cute that makes me weak in the knees. I've always had a thing for a studious man. There's something about the leather elbow pads, the smell of ink transferred to their skin from all the books they read.' She inhaled as though I reeked of it.

'You know what I imagined while lying in my bed at night?' She bobbed up and down, caught up in the moment.

'That a large pink machine was burrowing in your nether parts?'

She laughed. 'No, I thought about you, in your room next door, with your reading glasses on, a light over your shoulder, a book in your lap, and I wanted to barge in there and demand to know why you didn't find me sexy.'

'Impossible.' I let my head fall back.

'Don't look away. Watch me,' she commanded, although her voice was soft.

Pinching her nipples, she put on a show.

Seeing as there was nothing else I could do, I began to rock my pelvis, grinding my cock against her mound. Only the thin fabric of her panties, now slick with her desire,

193

separated us.

Her mouth closed down over mine and her tongue dove between my lips. Hard metal clacked against my teeth as the stud in her tongue swirled inside my mouth. Despite my initial shock, I soon relaxed under her care, giving as much as I received. She responded in turn, driving our passion up another level, matching my upward thrusts with her own downward ones. Eager for action, my hips danced of their own accord and before I knew it, I crested a plateau where there was no turning back.

My fingers gripped the sheets as my orgasm tore through me and I screamed out my pleasure with my tongue still in her mouth.

A moment later Elliot ceased all movement and pulled away.

That wasn't supposed to happen. We were supposed to go on for hours, or at the very least, she should have been satisfied.

I couldn't see her expression the way she sat looking down at the place where my release had darkened the material of her satin panties. All I could think was how mad and disappointed she must be feeling.

'I'm so sorry,' I said, certain I'd disappointed her. 'It's been …'

'A while,' she cut in, finishing for me. She raised her head and I was surprised to see her smiling. 'Trust me, I know.' With a brief wink of her eye she successfully baffled and flummoxed me again. 'Well, now that we have that out of the way …' She slid off the bed with a playful little bounce. I watched her cross the room and approach the spider dresser.

'What are you doing?' I asked, struggling to get out of my sleeves, but not having any luck.

'We needed to equal the playing field, as it were. You were a cannon, loaded and primed, with a lit fuse.' I stared at her perfectly pert bare bottom. 'And like I said, it's been a hard day. This is going to take a while.'

I saw her pick an item off the top of the dresser and pull two condoms out of a box just inside the top drawer.

Her hand gripped onto my softening cock.

'Oh!' I gasped. 'You don't waste any time, do you?'

'Not one second.' Her words slurred as she began tonguing the head.

I relaxed back onto the bed as her mouth slid down over my cock.

When I had grown satisfactorily hard once again she pushed me to my knees. I allowed her to position me so my head was level with the tops of her thigh highs, my mouth inches from her pussy.

Her hand went to the back of my head and a moment later my tongue was buried deep in the groove of her sex.

She stood over me while my mouth embraced her, my tongue teasing and lapping at her contours. I worked her clit, making her thighs tremble and her hands grip the back of my head. I didn't quit until she pulled my head back by the hair.

'Oh you did good, very, very good,' she said, seeming a little flushed in the cheeks.

She coaxed me into a standing position and before I knew what was happening I flinched as the cold surface of a condom touched my skin.

'Oh, we're going to have lots of fun, you and I.'

'You mean to say you won't need to replace your dildo any time too soon?'

'That depends.'

'On what?' I hadn't expected that.

'On how long you can go. After all, you did break my joy toy.' She spared me a sly wink before she knelt across the end of the bed.

I looked down at her presented bottom and remembered the endless hours of whirring. To keep up with that seemed daunting, but then I came to my senses when I thought about exactly what I'd be doing.

My gaze feasted upon the sight of her pussy, swollen and reddened with her desire.

'Then my punishment awaits.' I sank my cock deep into her pussy, knowing I'd satisfied far more than just my curiosity.

A Bonding Experience
by Teresa Noelle Roberts

'Carla, you're trembling,' Ryo whispered, as he hugged me.

I hadn't realised it myself. One of the scary things about Ryo is that he notices everything. I say scary for two reasons. One is that he's a top, and tops who read people really well are terrifyingly hot, or hotly terrifying.

The other is that Ryo's blind, but he's far more observant than most sighted people. It takes a little getting used to.

He drew me closer, making sure I felt his hard muscles, the strength of his arms – not to mention the stirring of his cock. His silky black hair caressed my face as he whispered in my ear, 'Thank you. I'll take it as a compliment.'

He drew his hands down my back, slowly and sensually, and murmured approval at the rope corset that cinched my waist and tormented my breasts. 'Nice,' he said. Then he kissed my forehead. It couldn't have been more chaste, but he imbued it with an intensity that made me shiver.

'Holding out my hand, Ryo,' my husband Erik said, extending his hand as he spoke. Instead of shaking hands, Ryo followed the voice to give Erik a big hug, a much quicker and rougher one than he'd given me, but just as affectionate. They were friends from college, but their history was more complicated – and sexier – than that phrase suggests.

I don't mean they'd been lovers. I'd flat-out asked Erik about that. He'd said no and he'd have no reason to lie to me about it. (It wasn't as if I'd be appalled. I'd just want details.) But Ryo had introduced Erik to rope bondage. The way they interacted, even now, had a sensei/student vibe to it, or maybe more like a dom/sub one, even though Erik was on the dom side of things himself. And Erik trusted Ryo enough that Ryo was the first person who got to beyond looking to touching in little games of voyeurism and exhibitionism we loved so much. Of course for Ryo, touching was looking, but checking out a lady's rope corset doesn't have to include giving her a bone-melting orgasm.

And today we were at Ryo's place, ostensibly so Erik could get a brush-up lesson on a particular bit of rope work.

It was likely to get very hands-on.

A voice said from behind Ryo, 'Come in, guys.' Ryo gestured us in and shut the door.

'Carla, Erik, this is Jessie.'

Did I mention Ryo's girlfriend was also going to be involved in the rope-bondage lesson? I hadn't met her yet. She did network security for some large company, but that was all I knew about her, other than that, like me, she liked how rope felt on her skin.

I wasn't sure what I expected Jessie to be like. I figured she'd be smart and eccentric, because that describes most of our friends, and kinky because Ryo definitely was. But to the extent I'd thought about her appearance, I'd figured she might be one of those seemingly plain girls with a bedroom voice and a sexy energy, the kind of things that might catch the attention of a guy who wouldn't notice a pretty face.

As it turned out, I was right about the bedroom voice and sexy energy. She sounded like some tragic jazz singer, sultry and suggestive even saying, 'Hello.'

I was wrong about the plain. Jessie's complexion was the colour of coffee and cream, her eyes were an unexpected green-hazel, striking with her dark skin, and she had the most perfect cheekbones I'd ever seen outside of the pages of a fashion magazine. Her hair clung in tight curls to her head, so short that I wanted to pet her like a cat, she sported a ruby stud in her nose, and she had a body like an ancient goddess, curvier than fashion, but strong and sensual. I imagined how much Ryo must enjoy tracing those well-muscled curves and I shivered internally.

At least I thought it was internal, but Jessie smiled at me then as if we shared a secret. Damn, if you could capture that smile, you could light up the city.

And if you could capture the throbbing going on between my legs – already pretty fierce from erotic anticipation, the rope corset under my clothes, and Ryo's caresses – you could probably take care of the suburbs too. I'm 80 per cent straight, but the other 20 per cent took this opportunity to remind me that I hadn't actually played with a woman since before Erik and I hooked up and it was high time to remedy that.

'Carla,' Jessie said, 'I'm so glad to meet you.' She held out her arms, inviting me to hug her.

No hesitation from my end. She felt as good as she looked, all curves, but with muscle underneath.

I could feel the rope corset, twin to my own, hidden beneath the oversized man's shirt she wore.

I wondered if her heart was beating double-time, like mine was. I wondered if she and Ryo played with other people a lot, and if she liked being shown off as much as I did.

I wondered if she liked girls.

And then I stopped wondering about the latter, because she was kissing me in a way that left no doubt the answer was yes.

And damn, that sensual mouth of hers could kiss.

Over the rush of hormones and the blood beating in my ears, I could hear Erik talking quietly. I knew he must be describing the kiss for Ryo. Erik's always been great at talking sexy, at describing a fantasy – or something more mundane, for that matter – so vividly I feel like I'm there. It occurred to me to wonder if he'd perfected that skill so Ryo could share in what he couldn't see.

Knowing we were being watched and described added fire to the kiss. I found my body squirming against Jessie's, my hands roaming eagerly. She was in a similar state.

All too soon, though, Erik's arms encircled my waist. He leaned in and whispered in my ear, 'Hey, save some for the rest of us.'

Ryo, less subtle, simply clasped his hand on the back of Jessie's neck, like you might do to an unruly kitten, and said, 'Down, girl! It's rude to monopolize our guest that way.'

'I'm sorry, Ryo.' Her voice sounded contrite, but she grinned and winked at me – an advantage of a blind partner – and she kept right on grinning when he smacked her ass.

'I'm not,' he countered, 'and I hope you're not.' The next sharp swat was hard enough to make her yelp. 'Because that would be rude too. I'm just trying to figure out how Erik and I can best use this to our advantage. The show's not as much fun for Erik if he has to describe it all, and using Braille will distract you.'

'More like make us hornier,' I threw in. We were already in trouble, if by trouble you mean 'about to be on the receiving end of some sexy so-called punishment that would end in fucking like lust-crazed weasels,' so I might as well keep fanning the flames.

'I have an idea.' Erik's voice dripped pure erotic evil. 'Let's tie them together, face to face. See how they like that.'

'Probably a lot,' Ryo said thoughtfully. 'So will we.' He hesitated only a second before saying – no, ordering – 'Jessie, strip.'

The command in his voice made me wetter than I had been, which was wet enough I was happy to get out of my jeans before they got sticky. I didn't wait for Erik to order me. Being naked suddenly seemed like the best idea I'd heard in a long time.

Erik ran his finger between my legs, chuckled at the thick strand of juice that followed it. 'She's dripping,' he said, glee in his voice.

'So is Jessie.' Ryo had bent Jessie over the arm of the couch and had two or maybe three fingers inside her. Jessie was making cat-in-heat noises and pushing back against him in a way that increased my own arousal.

I squirmed, hoping to convince Erik to stroke me some more. Instead, he laughed and pulled away. 'I've got rope in my pack,' he said.

'I'd rather use mine,' Ryo countered.

'Him and his hemp,' Jessie chuckled. 'Lucky us.'

'Bedroom's this way.'

The bedroom was as stark, yet comfortable, as I'd expect Ryo's bedroom to be – bare white walls, black lacquered four-poster bed, bare blonde wood floor. The bedspread, though, was a startling deep red, vivid in the otherwise neutral room. I bet Jessie picked it out, knowing that colour would set off Ryo's golden complexion.

And that was all I could tell you about the bedroom, because the guys pushed Jessie and me together – face to face, breast to breast, her thigh pressed between my legs, mine between hers – and I got a little distracted. All right, they didn't have to push very hard, and I was more than a little distracted. Jessie's tempting mouth was in easy kissing distance of mine and it took us almost no time to get back to what we'd been doing. Her lips seemed sweeter and hotter when we were skin to skin, her plump nipples teasing at mine, already sensitive from the rope corseting that restricted my breasts, her thigh pressing, grinding scrumptiously, against my aching clit and eager pussy.

'Should we take the rope corsets off?' Erik asked.

Ryo, who'd been busying himself with arranging skeins of natural-coloured hemp rope on the bed, moved behind Jessie, ran his hands over the rope work that cinched her waist and accentuated her breasts. 'Oh no, we'll work around them,' he said. Then he slipped his hands between our bodies to toy with her breasts. His knuckles grazed my nipples as he did. Heat flared through me.

'You're right,' Erik agreed, moving closer to enjoy the view. 'Leave the corset on.'

Ryo laughed and picked up the rope.

'Do we have a plan here?' Erik asked.

'Follow my lead,' Ryo replied. 'For once, I'm not going for elegance.'

We all laughed.

In my case, it turned into something more like a gasp of appreciation when Ryo crouched down by our side. I didn't know it was possible to squat gracefully, but he did.

And then he put rope against my skin and the gasp turned into a moan. My ankles aren't normally an erogenous zone, but if you put rope on them, I melt, thinking of all the wonderful ways I might be spread-eagled or teasingly restricted or otherwise gloriously, sexily controlled.

I'd never thought about how wonderful it would feel for rope to wrap from my ankles to another woman's, for us to be bound together. The rope, slightly coarse, yet infinitely sensual, gave me a million new nerve endings, all of them aware of the scent of Jessie's skin, the taste of her lips, the weight of her breasts against mine and the way her thigh twitched and rocked between my legs. Ryo's hands were cool and deft. He took his time, stroking our ankles and calves, arranging each loop and knot to an alignment that suited him. Jessie and I alternated between kissing frantically and pausing to appreciate Ryo's handiwork, the new, exquisite restrictions being placed on us.

He pressed his lips to the back of Jessie's knee. She let out a sweet, soft noise that made me wetter than I already was.

That sound apparently galvanized Erik. He'd seemed content to watch, idly stroking his cock through his jeans at the pretty sight. Now he took up a second hank of rope and

202

crossed to stand behind me. 'Hey, beautiful,' he whispered, and nibbled my ear. He worked his way down to my shoulder, kissing and nipping and sending jolts of pleasure through me. It distracted me from what his hands were doing.

I didn't realise until he moved, trailing rope over my skin and Jessie's as he did, that he'd tied Jessie's hands together behind my back.

Now he was going to do the same to me.

I froze, almost unable to breath. He looped the rope around my wrists, a simple, casual tie we'd used a hundred times. I always enjoyed it, always revelled in the paradox of how free I felt when I was tied. But knowing I was now bound to Jessie like this, that I couldn't let go of her in the unlikely event I wanted to, made me lose my mind.

All the while, Ryo's hands and ropes were working their way up our legs, weaving a spell. The ropes pulled us even closer together making it impossible to think about anything but Jessie, Ryo, Erik and the rope itself.

Erik walked around us, veering out so he didn't interfere with what Ryo was doing. He secured the rope and repeated the circumnavigation of Planet Horny Women, working a little lower this time.

Jessie was slick against me, drenching my thigh with her juices. I rocked my hips as best I could, moved my leg between hers as she was doing for me. It was getting harder to move at all, between the ropes and the fog of desire that surrounded me. But the restriction only made me hotter. As for Jessie, her eyes were closed, her lips were parted, and she was moaning and gasping and mewling steadily, the symphony of sounds adding to my arousal.

In contrast, the guys were unnervingly quiet. I'd have thought they'd need to discuss what they were doing, but they worked with only a few words, most of them along the lines of, 'Excuse me,' or, 'Pretty!'

After a while, Ryo stopped what he was doing to inspect

Erik's work – which, of course, meant running his hands all over Jessie's body and mine. 'You're getting a little sloppy,' he teased, 'but I bet the girls are too.'

He tested his theory on Jessie, reaching between her legs from behind to test her wetness. Erik, no slouch, did the same to me. He couldn't reach my clit because of the way Jessie and I were intertwined, but he stroked my pussy lips, teased the rim of my anus until I was gasping and begging and bucking as best I could against his hand – and of course, against Jessie.

Which only added to the sensations Ryo was giving her and Erik was giving me. Add to that the hemp rope on our skin, the endless kissing and constant contact, the knowledge that we were appreciated and loved and a treat for Ryo and Erik's senses, and what few brain cells I had gave up the fight.

Waves of pure, liquid sensation crashed over me. I bucked and trembled and cried out a word that didn't exist in any language but would be recognised in any of them. My frantic movements must have been the last bit of stimulation that Jessie needed, because she began to thrash as well, her cries high and quivering. Her juices gushed onto my thigh, and that set me off again.

At some point during the time we writhed against each other, the ropes must have started to loosen. I can't say when, because I was caught in another wave of orgasm and probably would have missed it if the ceiling caved in. But by the time my brain came back online, the pretty bondage was definitely unravelling. Erik's gave way first, leaving our hands tied in place, but our torsos unbound and a lot of rope coiled on the floor at our feet. Ryo's handiwork didn't fall apart quite as dramatically, but it was sagging down our legs because he hadn't had a chance to weave it into Erik's web.

Ryo shook his head in mock dismay. 'All that work for nothing!'

'Nothing?' Erik asked. 'Weren't you the one who always

said the real point of rope work was a wet, writhing, orgasmic woman? Looks like we've done a fine job.'

Ryo nodded thoughtfully. 'But the ropes are getting all tangled now. There's only one thing to do.'

'Which is?' Erik asked. I swear they rehearsed it.

'We finish untying them and then we and our respective ladies have wild monkey sex. If they don't mind a little seeing and being seen, that is.'

We didn't. We especially didn't mind Ryo's Braille version of voyeurism.

But that's another story.

Like Ribbons
by L A Fields

Missy flips her braid over her shoulder and gets serious. It's not like her to be shy. If she's going to proposition one of the boys lanking around the street, she should just do it and quit staring at them. It's rude and unattractive to stand around and gawk.

Missy has her eye on one in particular: a skinny shaggy-haired kid. She needs to cross the street with enough insouciance so it doesn't look like she's buying. *This ain't a fruit stand*, she tells herself, but then starts laughing, because it kind of is too. She doubts these boys get approached by women very often, and girls such as herself must be unseen in their line of work. It's not that Missy can't get laid on her own, she often does, but this one boy is so arresting, and she's a modern gal, and she could use a story about how one time she picked up a prostitute in Phoenix, for her reputation. She can do this.

Missy looks both ways (safety first!) before sort of meandering across the road. It's midday, almost too hot to be out in the street, but she supposes that hustlers are like mail carriers: neither rain, nor sleet, nor dark of night, nor baking freaking desert sun keeps them from their appointed rounds. It feels strange to be doing something so shady and illegal in the middle of the blazing day like this, but Missy supposes all evil can't happen at night.

She wanders by her boy, looking at the ground mostly, and ends up accidentally on purpose leaning against the same telephone pole as him. He gives her a quick up-and-down, and so do some of the others in this loose cluster. Missy is used to feeling eyes rove over her, but this is even more critical a gaze than she gets from guys in bars. They probably think she's here to display her wares as well, and perhaps they're feeling encroached upon. Missy decides to make her intentions clear right away.

'Hi,' she says to the boy. He looks at her again, very quickly, and then back out at the passing cars. Missy has her next line rehearsed. 'What can I do to earn the pleasure of your company?'

The boy starts, and looks at her more closely. That was probably a weird way to put it, but Missy is new at this and bound to be a little heavy-handed.

'It's just you?' the boy asks. Missy nods, glad that he's finally looking right at her, because she can see his pretty eyes. 'You're not out shopping for a boyfriend or a pimp or somebody?' Missy shakes her head. The boy makes a "whatever" face and even starts to smile a little. 'I accept gifts and donations of no less than $50,' he says.

'I've got that,' she says. 'I'm in a loft right down the street.'

'We can go there?' the boy asks. Missy nods again. 'OK,' he says. 'Lead the way.'

Walking through the industrial section of town, turning every now and again to make sure the boy is keeping up, Missy is suddenly very impatient. She and the other two members of her band are crashing in someone's flop-house of a loft while he's up to his own trouble, and for the next few hours Missy has the place to herself while the boys are out getting their van worked on. For some reason the assumption was that a girl would be dead weight at a garage, which is absolutely false, since she could at least have flirted up a discount, but she wanted them out of her hair for a while anyway, and she is never above using sexism to her advantage.

208

Inside, their borrowed place isn't that spectacular. Hardly any furniture; just mattresses and milk crates, a dumpster couch, bare walls, and a TV that still needs an antennae. The boy doesn't seem to notice. He and Missy stare at each other expectantly for a moment before she says, 'Right, the money,' and hurries off to get it. She locks the bedroom door before digging out 50 bucks from her purse. *Just because he's cute doesn't mean he won't rob you*, she thinks. Words to live by.

But he's right where she left him when she hands him the money, and for a beat they stare awkwardly again. This time he says, 'I've never been with a girl before. I hope you don't mind.'

'Not at all,' Missy says smiling. She likes being someone's first girl. 'Does that mean you're gay when you're not doing this?' she asks. He nods. 'I figured. I always think the gay ones are cute.'

His face cocks in a tiny smile, and a tingle runs through Missy. She reaches up and pulls down the spaghetti straps of her flowery sun dress and lets it shimmy to the floor. Her skin flushes as the boy looks at her, and suddenly it's less about him and more about having an audience. She unclasps her strapless bra and lets her full Cs push it off on their own. She's got her panties halfway to her knees before the boy even thinks to pull off his shirt. But he's naked soon enough, and even a little hard, flatteringly.

Missy takes his hands, cups them on her breasts, and then leads the boy to the couch she wants to do it on. She finally asks him for his name.

'I'm Wade,' he says, sitting down where she sets him. He's become very pliable, and Missy wonders what he's like with the men who pick him up, whether that's who he really is in bed or if it's something he has cultivated for business purposes.

'I'm Missy,' she tells him. 'And I like to be on top. Is that OK?' Wade nods, and she urges him to lie back. On the end crate (the end table made out of a milk crate), is a little dish of condoms. Missy and her lead guitar get laid way too often to have the condoms sequestered away in a bathroom drawer. They lay them out like candy at Grandma's.

Missy picks up Wade Junior like it's a mouse with a broken leg, gently, gently. She feels a pulse of blood jump through and is pleased. No one as young as Wade is ever all that gay. She's gotten physical responses from a lot of self-professed gay boys; girl or guy, a good blow job is hard to ignore.

And to prove the point, Missy applies the condom with her mouth, and keeps at it until Wade has reached maximum density. Then she saddles up on him, pausing before the main event to feel the heat spread out from between her legs, to run her hands over Wade's chest, and to let down her extremely long, gingery hair so that it will tickle and cascade over her skin.

Wade slides in easily, because at this point she's incredibly turned on. Her mouth is hanging open, and she wants to ask for a kiss, but doesn't know how fair that would be, so she goes for Wade's earlobe instead, just to have something in her mouth.

Missy does, however, feel comfortable asking Wade to suck on her nipple. She once had a guy tell her they looked delicious, like inverted strawberries on mounds of vanilla ice cream, the poet. Missy herself can reach the things with her mouth, which thrills certain guys no end, though surely Wade would be unimpressed.

He knows what he's doing however, nuzzling and lipping around her breasts, giving her a little gasping thrill, like being splashed with cold water. Eventually she can feel the approaching peak, and she leans back, getting a better angle on her pleasure, and with the aid of her hand she ultimately cinches around an orgasm.

Missy stays still for a moment, perched atop Wade, and he

210

can feel her insides fluttering as the twitching of her muscles dies down slowly. She eases herself off him and pulls back at least a yard of coppery hair.

'Do you wanna come?' she says, and it's sweet of her to ask, but Wade shakes his head.

'I should probably go,' he tells her. This has been OK, relatively, but it's always weird fucking strangers for money, and he doesn't make a habit of hanging around to be friends afterwards. It's just good business.

Missy peels the condom off and Wade's dick kind of lays down, like it's tired from all the excitement. Missy grabs her dress and goes to flush the condom, coming back as the dress falls down over her naked body. She's one of those Botticelli girls, fleshy, but in a hips and breasts kind of way. If he were straight, Wade decides, he'd probably be into it. As it is, he's pulling his pants up over a windsock.

'You're welcome to stay and hang out,' Missy says as they hear the huge clanky elevator start up. 'That'll be the guys.' She kicks her underwear beneath the couch, and smiles at Wade. 'You might like Darian. I know Darian would like you.'

Wade hesitates while pulling his shirt down over his ears, wondering if he heard right, wondering if it might be possible. 'Who?' he asks.

'Darian. He's my band mate. Darian's on guitar, I'm on keyboard, Aaron's on drums.'

Wade is remembering, his brain time-tripping violently. His Darian played guitar. His Darian once picked him up out of North Carolina and introduced him to a life that, for all its ups and downs and standing on street corners peddling his ass, is one he wouldn't have missed for anything.

'What's his last name?' Wade asks.

Missy's eyes narrow, like she too can feel the rumble of strange coincidence in the air. 'Darian Jule,' she says, watching Wade's face for signs of recognition, which are evident immediately. It *is* Darian. It's been so long.

211

The front door opens, and first in with some grocery bags is a mousy kid with dirty smudges on his face who looks sad when he sees a strange guy in the room. Next through the door is a guy who was once the sun to Wade, his hero, his role model, a guy who long ago got cast in bronze for Wade, an ideal to be reached for though never achieved.

'Darian,' he says. And Missy with an ironic smirk on her mouth says, 'I believe you two have met.' She takes the grocery bags from Darian's dangling hands and ushers the other guy into the kitchen. Darian stands looking at Wade, just as tall and gorgeous as ever. Even with his mouth slack and stupid, trying to place the face before him, Wade can tell he still has that same charming smile.

'Wade Anderson,' Darian says slowly, his smile coming out to play. 'How's your mother?'

Wade laughs and rushes into a hug so big it lifts him off the ground, and Wade's not the kid he used to be, so it's a bit of a feat. Their lips meet as a matter of course, and even though it's been nearly four years since their last kiss, for Wade it's like waking up; it feels like he's been asleep for ever, but nothing you can remember is that far away.

'What are you doing here?' Darian asks, and Wade hardly hears him because he smells exactly the same, and Wade is still reeling from the clash of his past with his present.

'It's …' he hesitates as his history catches up with him. The memories from the day he just lived flood in, rightfully superseding the ones from that summer when he and Darian met by happy accident on the road. He remembers getting picked up by a girl, of all unlikely things, and losing his heterosexual virginity to a friend of the guy who claimed him first. 'It's kind of a funny story,' he says. 'And it's kind of a long one too.'

Hours later, Wade is still talking. He's got a little story-time circle audience made out of Darian, Missy, and Aaron, the mousy guy. They keep asking question like curious children, which is strange, because Wade's definitely the youngest one in the room. They want to know about the whole prostitution thing.

'It's not something I do all the time,' he tells them. 'Just when I get stranded without money. It's usually pretty easy to spot the hot street and just hang around for a while.'

They want to know about his clientele, but he won't tell them about every John, Dick and Mary who's ever picked him up, just the interesting ones. He had a date once take him shopping at a sex store for an assortment of toys Wade would allow the guy to use on him, and he got to keep the stuff afterwards, which was just sweet and hygienic of the man. He had one really boring encounter with a guy who ended up being a school principle, since Wade noticed the parking tag hanging from his rear view mirror. He'd been trying to place the smell on the guy, the scent of hallways and warm printer paper.

Wade tells about the few guys who were red flags, that he didn't go home with. One offered him double his usual rate to fuck him without a condom, and Wade could just not imagine a scenario where the guy wouldn't try to do it anyway, even though Wade refused. He also got rolled by a cop once, since why else would the guy be so particular in trying to get Wade to say that his minimum gift or donation fee was explicitly for the payment of sex acts. Nice try.

Eventually Aaron and Missy retire (to the same bedroom, the same bed, but Wade doesn't ask any questions), and only Darian is left. He was sitting on the floor for story-time, but he gets up and sits close to Wade on the couch. Needlessly close. They take up a cushion and a half on a three-person sofa. Wade can feel his expression going all doe-eyed and tries to tamp it down. He likes Darian, but he's not 15 any more. There's no reason to start hero-worshiping again.

'You'll hang out for a while, won't you?' Darian asks. 'Stay the night?'

'Sure,' Wade says, and after a quiet second, he kisses

213

Darian on the mouth. Time pitches again, and he can feel the kid he used to be trying to squeeze in next to who he's become more recently. Suddenly Wade is not so sure he wants to stick around. It isn't a bad feeling, or at least he can't tell yet, but it's uncomfortable. He's just not himself today.

Darian's bedroom is off the main hallway, and he is as lost as Wade is in the dark, this being only temporary housing. The van is where they truly live most days, but when it needs to be in an auto garage overnight, they take what they can get.

Rather than turn on a light switch, Darian prefers to feel his way, first to the bed and then over Wade's body. He too is throwing himself through time warps, imagining at times that he is with the Wade he remembers, and then switching abruptly to the Wade he met today. He not only looks different – he's taller, his hair is longer, his posture and movement have matured – but it's as if he's altered from the inside out. Wade used to be inexhaustible, and now he has a new lethargy. His eyes were once open and naïve, and now they are more lidded, learned, older. Darian feels like it hasn't been long enough for anyone to change so much, but kids grow up so fast these days.

And not everything is different either. Wade still kisses the same, with a strange up-and-down movement of his jaw, like he's chewing. And he still looks at Darian the same way, like he can't believe his luck. Darian remembers picking up a kid who started hitchhiking one day out of boredom, who didn't know who he was or what he was doing. Darian has been with a lot of guys, and in fact he and Missy have a friendly rivalry in most towns trying to pick people up, but this is an absolute first. He'll be with people off and on over the years, but Darian has never had to meet the same guy twice.

'I feel weird,' Wade says after Darian strips off his shirt

214

and is smoothing Wade's hair back off his face. His bones stand out more. He's lost the baby fat around his cheeks. He's still pretty cute though.

'I think you feel fine,' Darian says. Wade rolls his eyes a little, but Darian's smile takes the edge off his lame line. A friend of his from college, another musician, once told him his smile could only be measured in kilowatts. Wade seems just as blinded.

'You never came back for me,' Wade says, and now he looks like the boy Darian remembers, the boy he left at his mother's house in North Carolina when it was the right thing to do.

'I did,' Darian says. 'I came back the very next summer. Your mom said you'd disappeared again. When'd you make running away a habit?'

'The day I met you,' Wade admits. 'I was so lucky the first time I figured I'd try again.'

Darian nods, his head falling against Wade's chest, kissing him lightly. It sounds like a sad song. Darian can imagine what happened. Wade ran away once just on a lark, and got to spend a few weeks in the relative paradise of Darian's van (anything's better than high school), and got a taste for something he could never recreate. Even now that they've met again, it's just not the same. Wade's not the same. All his searching has changed him.

They end up sleeping together, but not having sex, and in the morning Wade and Darian trade cell phones, inputting their number for the other. They each become a name in a long list of guys, and Wade has to put the abbreviation NC after his name, because at this point Darian keeps track of boys by state. He and Missy both keep their address books in such a manner, trying to avoid confusion. She's around when Wade leaves, remaining at a discreet distance until he and Darian can hug and kiss and say goodbye in peace, and then she's there, an impeccable friend.

'Do you miss this one?' Missy asks, as they move to the

window to watch Wade leave the building, walking down the street with an acquired gait, not at all the bouncy way he used to move.

'A little bit more now that we've been reunited.'

Missy nods sagely. Aaron doesn't get around as much, or really at all. He doesn't know what it's like having all these memories of past lovers trailing out behind you, but Missy gets it, and probably Wade does too.

Lonely whistling as it goes, the cracked back windows, the car, he knows ... You're losing something all the time. One of the first songs Darian and Missy wrote together, a folksy acoustic thing that sealed their band together and made them realise they were the same kind of person, that they shared some kind of truth. The lyrics go on just as Missy says, 'No matter where you're headed, you're leaving someone else behind.'

She claps him on the shoulder, and says it's just about time to hit the road again.

Also from Xcite Books

Ultimate Uniforms

If a commanding man or imperious woman dressed in a smart uniform makes your heart tick faster, these 20 original stories exploring the sensual delights of uniforms, both for the wearer and the admirer, are guaranteed to seize your attention.

Whether it is the smartness and authority of military dress, the sassy temptations of a naughty maid, or the possibilities offered by a policewoman, arousing descriptions and unabashed accounts of kinky sexual encounters await!

ISBN 9781907761324   £7.99

Xcite Books help make loving better
with a wide range of erotic books,
eBooks and dating sites.

www.xcitebooks.com
www.xcitebooks.co.uk
www.xcitebooks.com.au

Sign up to our Facebook page
for special offers and free gifts!